'Quin works over a small area with the finest of tools. Every page, every word gives evidence of her care and workmanship.'

New York Times

'Quin's prose never falters.'

Caitlin Youngquist, *Paris Review*

'Vividly intense and almost palpably immediate.'

Irish Times

'The most naturally and delicately gifted novelist of her generation.'

The Scotsman

'Quin was a writer ahead of her time.'

Publishers Weekly

'One of Britain's most adventurous post-war writers. Psychologically dark and sexually daring, Quin's fearlessly innovative prose reads like nobody else.'

Juliet Jacques

'Quin understood she was on to something new and she took herself seriously, in the right way; she had a serious sense of her literary purpose.'

Deborah Levy

'Despite ongoing rumours of a B.S. Johnson revival, I feel our attention could be more usefully directed towards Ann Quin.'

Stewart Home, in *69 Things to do with a Dead Princess*

THE UNMAPPED COUNTRY

STORIES AND FRAGMENTS

Ann Quin

Edited and Introduced
by Jennifer Hodgson

SHEFFIELD – LONDON – NEW HAVEN

First published in 2018 by And Other Stories
Sheffield – London – New Haven
www.andotherstories.org

Some of the stories and fragments in this collection are previously unpublished and some have already been published. For fuller detail, see the Note on Sources at the end of the collection.

9 8 7 6 5 4 3 2

ISBN: 978-1-911508-14-4
eBook ISBN: 978-1-911508-15-1

Editor: Jennifer Hodgson; Proofreader: Sarah Terry; Typesetter: Tetragon, London; Typefaces: Linotype Swift Neue and Verlag; Cover Design: Edward Bettison. Printed and bound by the CPI Group (UK) Ltd, Croydon, CRO 4YY.

A catalogue record for this book is available from the British Library.

This book was supported using public funding by Arts Council England.

CONTENTS

INTRODUCTION

Ann Quin was a rare breed in British writing: radically experimental, working class and a woman. The author of four novels and a prolific writer of short stories and fragments (as well as memoir, poetry, and radio and television plays), she was born in Brighton in 1936 to what used to be called an unmarried mother. In 'Leaving School – XI', a piece of memoir-writing collected in this volume, she writes of her 'sense of sin' and 'great lust to find out', which took her to London, where she worked as a secretary by day and wrote her strange, singular novels by night – typewriter clattering away into the early hours. A newspaper profile from 1965 describes her 'marvellously cluttered' bed-sitting room in Notting Hill Gate: the walls are a pasted-up montage of torn pages from magazines and art postcards – painters, playwrights, French film stars. Shelves teem with paperbacks, there's her typewriter, of course, and a collection of esoteric knick-knacks. It's clear that her sights are set far beyond the hot-water bottle, gas ring and candlewick bedspread of this L-shaped room. Like other restless English writers before her, Quin embarked on a search for the spiritual antipodes of her homeland, which she depicts in her writing as buttoned-up, repressed and mildewed around the edges.

Quin was part of a remarkable coterie of innovative writers that emerged in Britain during the 1960s, including BS Johnson, Christine Brooke-Rose, Brigid Brophy, Alan Burns, Robert Nye and others. Her stories and fragments are murky, voyeuristic and formally off-kilter, filled with sudden blazes of intensity, occult images and erotic artifice. Stylistically, they run the gamut from expressionist renditions that blur memory, perception and fantasy to Burroughsian cut/up and montage. Certain preoccupations, though, emerge again and again: mingled voices, tensions between thinking and feeling, dysfunctional families and transgenerational disquiet, febrile and free-flowing desires that are always in the end thwarted, conversations that seem to say nothing whatsoever but somehow reveal everything.

The stories collected in this volume span the course of Quin's writing career. The earliest, 'B.B.'s Second Manifesto' and 'Untitled', were written around 1962, prior to the publication of her debut novel, the seaside noir, *Berg* (1964). They were ghosted on behalf of her then-lover, the New Zealand pop artist, Billy Apple, and reflect the art school's abiding influence upon her. At the time, she worked as a secretary at the Royal College of Art, where she encountered the British pop art scene that was incubating there amongst artists like David Hockney, Peter Blake, Pauline Boty, Patrick Caulfield and others. Pop's phantasmic vision of Amerika, and its techniques of subverting the styles and iconography of the mass media, would come to preoccupy her later work, and especially the short stories 'Living in the Present' and 'Tripticks', the latter of which seeded her final published novel of the same name.

Impressively, Quin parlayed the promise and warm reception of *Berg* into an extraordinary freewheeling existence, living, loving and writing her own picaresque. She wrote three more novels in the years that followed: *Three* (1966), *Passages* (1969) and *Tripticks* (1972). Perpetually broke, she lived hand to mouth off her publisher's advances, the occasional Arts Council grant or university fellowship to fund extended trips to Ireland, Greece, the United States, the Bahamas and Mexico. In the press profiles of her that appeared at the time, one can almost detect the licking of journalists' stiff upper lips when confronted by this 'Miss Quin', with her 'shapely legs' and candid reflections upon her peripatetic lifestyle, unconventional relationships and experiments with drugs. In the States, she immersed herself in the alternative living scene and found a sort of home-in-exile amongst the American post-Beat poets, forming relationships with two of them (Robert Creeley and Robert Sward) and driving across the mesa from New Mexico to attend the Berkeley Poetry Congress. In her writing, as in her life, Quin is often drawn to experiences of difference, extremity and disorientation. The stories 'Never Trust a Man Who Bathes with his Fingernails',

'Eyes That Watch Behind the Wind' and 'Ghostworm' place her protagonists in landscapes at once sensuous and brutal, confronting alienatingly unfamiliar cultures, or else tasked with the dangerous and delicious risks of transgressing social prohibitions. They seek, as she writes in 'Ghostworm', 'EXPERIENCE in caps period', to 'live beyond' the confines of the self. But equally, despite (because of?) her ambivalence towards home, Quin is peculiarly attuned to the grotesque details, to what she calls the 'eggy mouthcorners' of ordinary life. 'A Double Room' and 'Every Cripple Has His Own Way of Walking', especially, are redolent of greasy mackintoshes, milk skin, of bare, swinging light bulbs, of chintz and clag.

Increasingly, though, towards the end of her life, Quin found herself having wandered too far off the map. She died young, swimming out to sea near Brighton's Palace Pier in 1973 when she was 37. She had been due, later that year, to take up a place on the University of East Anglia's prestigious creative writing course. Suffering frequent and devastating bouts of mental illness, she spent periods in psychiatric institutions and underwent electroconvulsive therapy (ECT). Her final novel, 'The Unmapped Country', which remained unfinished at the time of her death, draws upon these experiences for its trenchant critique of mental health care. Elsewhere, her writing explores the risks and seductions of going over the edge; this final work is about the horrors of 'going sane'.

In 'The Unmapped Country', the protagonist Sandra criticises artists' and writers' 'need for posterity'. 'How much better,' she decides, 'to create like the Navajo Indians, beginning at sunrise in the desert, a sand painting that would be rubbed out by sundown.' But although partial to the romance of ephemeral art, Quin clearly didn't intend a similar fate for her own work. As a 'cult' author, her influence is difficult to point to with certainty – though China Miéville and Deborah Levy have recently paid homage to her. That said, there's a kinship between Quin and some of the most audacious writing of the twentieth century and beyond.

Her work bridges the world of modernists such as Virginia Woolf, Elizabeth Bowen and Anna Kavan with what came after. She would have been quite at home amongst the women avant-gardists of the 1980s and 90s like Kathy Acker and Chris Kraus. And there's something distinctly Quin-like about the riskiness, the subversive joy in confronting the subterranean aspects of human experience present in many of the most interesting contemporary writers: Eimear McBride, Claire-Louise Bennett, Anakana Schofield, Sheila Heti, Levy herself, and others.

In letters from the mid-sixties to her publisher, Marion Boyars of Calder and Boyars, whose list at the time comprised some of the most cosmopolitan and provocative writing of the period, Quin mentions 'writing short stories at a fantastic rate'. It's clear that she was energised by turning her hand to the form: 'the short story medium is something new, exciting,' she writes, comparing the 'curved shape' of the short story to the 'spiral' of the novel, enthusing about the 'space for readers to explore'. Perhaps it's no surprise that this fiction writer who called herself a poet, and whose work is so much concerned with moments, glances, shifting moods, scenes flickering in and out of view, should find herself comfortable here, in the closer, headier confines of short fiction. The stories collected here for the first time distil Quin at her wildest and often her most virtuosic. And collectively they demonstrate, in rare and unexpected ways, an imagination committed to pushing British fiction into weirder, dirtier and more anarchic places.

JENNIFER HODGSON

THE UNMAPPED COUNTRY

Bound by perverse securities in a convent, RC Brighton for eight years. Taking that long to get over. The Holy Ghost. The Trinity. The Reverend Mother. I was not a Catholic. I was sent to a convent to be brought up 'a lady'. To say gate and not giate – the Sussex accent I had picked up from the village school in my belly-rubbing days had to be eliminated by How Now Brown Cow, if I wanted to make my way in the world. According to Mother.

Non-Catholics attended chapel every Friday. Joined in the morning prayers. Hymns. Marched in the Corpus Christi processions, dressed in white, knelt on hot tennis courts, but not allowed to throw petals. Listened to scripture lessons. Struggled up from desk at noon and mumbled the Angelus. At fourteen I wanted Heaven and Hell to be defined, never believing in Hell fire, nor that Heaven consisted of being completely content looking at an old man, white-haired, bearded, called God. Limbo always made more sense. Not being baptized, that was where my soul, uncleansed from Original Sin, would end up. I believed in that then.

Enclosed by grey walls. Were they grey? Corridors. Women fettered from head to toe in black and white. Their white faces. Did they use rice powder for such an effect? Black habits whispering. Sound of bells. Rosaries. Holy pictures exchanged. Statues and candles. Sun caught in the chalice. Did they use real blood? Impact of wooden pews. The devil was close, hiding in the folds of black gowns. Cracks of playground. He grinned from the shadows between statues, and was secretly conjured up, after school, on the Downs. Christ was distant, wearing his crown of thorns, body bleeding. He had redeemed every one of us. Hail Mary Full of Grace looked so sorrowful I felt more pity for her. Christ after all had been made in the image of man, and men were to be distrusted. Life was but a preparation for the greater life hereafter. A ritualistic culture that gave me a conscience. A death wish and a sense of sin. Also a great lust to find out, experience what evil really was.

Weekdays I sleepwalked through. Evenings spent in reading; half-heartedly doing homework, preferring to explore books discovered in the Public Library: Greek and Elizabethan dramatists. Dostoievsky (*Crime and Punishment*, and Virginia Woolf's *The Waves* made me aware of the possibilities in writing). Chekhov, Lawrence, Hardy, etc., rather than learning the coal fields. The Corn Law. Amo, amas, amat. 'Ode To A Nightingale' off by heart. Irregular verbs. More fascinated by the colour of Mademoiselle's bloomers. The way her face shrivelled, changed from ash to the colour of her bloomers, than her attempts to manipulate my mouth into an uuuuuuuuu. More stimulated by the girl who had a crush on me, than hearing about the Poor Law. More worried about my stained gym slip growing up my limbs to meet my navy blue knickers, than chalk marks on the blackboard dealing with measurement, relationship of points, lines, angles, surfaces and solids. More curious by what the nuns wore in bed. If they were really bald. If they stripped completely for a bath, than split infinitives. More excited in getting into the Sixth Form, not only because the classroom windows overlooked the boys' college, but on the whole sinful world that lay before me at the end of the year. That world at seventeen consisted mainly of the theatre, having spent every Saturday queuing up for a seat in the Gods at the Theatre Royal to witness a fantasy world that relieved my many desires, frustrations. I decided to go on the stage. I longed for rôles that would suit my varied moods, and for an immediate audience. I had been writing stories since the age of seven to entertain myself, and writing in comparison to acting seemed such a solitary occupation. I lived in a dream world and created dreams out of everyday situations until nothing ever seemed what it appeared to be. At fourteen I met my half brother for the first time and fell desperately in love with him; he died five years later and I saw myself as Antigone. At eighteen I went up to London to spend Saturdays with my father (he had left my mother when I was ten) and pretended he was my lover.

I passed the GCE in one subject: English language. I failed in literature. Half the paper was based on *The Tempest*, which we had done for an end-of-term production, I had played Caliban; I filled the exam paper with Caliban's speeches, and philosophized on his good and evil aspects. So at sweet seventeen and never been… I passed through the Gates of Eden. Threw away my uniform, thick lisle stockings, wore makeup every day, bought high heels, nylons, and joined a Rep. Company as an ASM. Pocket money spent on the train fares. I worked from 8:30 a.m. to 11 p.m. Collected props from sceptical antique dealers. Scrubbed the stage, where I recited Shakespeare, if no one was around. Sewed costumes. Made tea, coffee. Shifted scenery. Knocked on dressing room doors, and stood back in envy, awe, as the cast transformed themselves. And attempted to laugh at the camp jokes I didn't understand. During lunch breaks I ate sandwiches, made up poems, in a church nearby. Six weeks spent hanging between what I had anticipated, and clinging to what had been known within the convent walls.

I had a row with the stage manager. I think it was over the hem of a costume I had sewn crooked (only ever having done embroidery). I was asked to leave. I left in tears. Back to the world of books, and efforts to have some kind of social life with 'people of my own age'. I joined the Young Conservatives' Association, and sat in the Grand Hotel on a Saturday night, dressed in long white, next to a similar wallflower friend, longing for a

Paul Jones, and when that came, my partner would be shorter, fatter, breathe down my neck and step on my toes. I sold my soul to the devil for a Heathcliff, and to be rich and famous. I wrote inspired poems in the middle of the night, mainly religious and surrealistic. I won a poetry prize. The devil had obviously accepted my offer. When I arrived to collect the prize, a 10s. book token, I was greeted by half a dozen very old dears, some in wheelchairs, who clapped enthusiastically after I read my sonnet, called 'The Lost Seagull' – about gulls being damned souls.

Still interested in going on the stage, I tried getting into RADA. I learned two pieces for the audition. I expected a stage, even a platform, instead a smallish room, brightly lit; ten or twelve people faced me. I began, froze, asked to start again, but was struck dumb, and rushed out, silently screaming down Gower Street. I would be a writer. A poet. Where what I had to express, say, would be my own interpretation, my own vision and be accepted by an unseen audience.

I took a secretarial course, and only my determination that it would be a means towards bread and butter, kept me at this for a year. Armed with shorthand and typewriting certificates I went to a secretarial agency in London, and got a job in a newspaper office, a small concern, but in Fleet Street. I got up at 6 a.m. to catch the train, and would be back at 8 p.m. thoroughly exhausted. A nightmare that was extended by the editor hanging himself in a cupboard, who left a note beside the whisky bottle to the effect he had contemplated suicide for forty years. Soon after, thankfully, I had appendicitis. Not very keen on getting another job I prolonged convalescence, and took a part-time course in painting. I had noticed a Heathcliff walking along the seafront, who was obviously an art student. The devil was apparently still acknowledging me. I fell in love, and that world merged with what I had seen at the theatre, what I had read, until nothing, no one else existed. I wrote more poems, less religious, started a journal, and wrote beautiful love letters.

Eventually I took a job in a solicitor's office in Brighton. Again days spent in sleepwalking, through Abstract of Titles; letters that never varied. But the world of love awaited me every evening, I lived for that, would have gladly died for it. The job, the love lasted two years.

Heart-broken I tackled London again. I got a job as a secretary in the foreign rights department of a publishing firm. Found a room in Soho, and began my first novel, called *A Slice of the Moon*, about a homosexual, though at the time I had never met one, knew very little about queers (maybe I had read something on Proust?). The salary I earned was barely enough for rent and food. In winter I lived on potatoes, saved on the gas fire by going to bed, hotwaterbottled, typewriter balanced on knees. I rarely went out in the evenings, but was a voyeur, in the sense of watching from my window the prostitutes, and became fascinated by a blonde one, by the type of men she picked up, they all seemed the same in their fawn raincoats, trilbies, the same age. I timed her by watching for the light in her room to go on, off. Never longer than ten minutes. I contemplated what an easier existence I might have by doing similar work, earning in one day what I received from my job at the publishers in a week. However, I continued going into the office, a whale's mouth of a place, small window overlooked fire escape. Days spent in typing out contracts, answering the telephone, taking letters and so on. And going back every evening to my novel. A time when I worked the hardest at writing, more disciplined than I have ever done since. This lasted eighteen months or more.

I decided to go back to Brighton, live at home, and take a part-time job, while finishing the book. I worked at St Dunstan's, in the office, but as there was very little work there, I also took the blind men out – or rather they took me out: straight to the nearest pub, it was up to me to bring them safely back. After one episode of leading two blind men, one either side of me, on to the grass verge, they precariously balanced on the bank, shouting, waving their sticks, thinking I had led them to the cliff edge, I gave the job up. The novel finished I sent it off to a publisher. Rejected. I sent it off to another publisher, likewise rejected. I put it away, and began another book.

Back in London, I took a part-time job in a solicitor's office: three days a week, and began a social life of allowing men to wine and dine me (I'd had enough of potatoes – besides they made me fatter) but somewhat guiltily refused to invite them up for coffee afterwards. I fell in love with poverty-stricken painters, who needed feeding as much as I did, so that never lasted long. I spent a winter, spring, doing office work in a noisy basement, and decided I couldn't face the summer there, so applied for a hotel job in Cornwall.

Bearing books, half-finished novel, I arrived at the hotel. The setup there consisted of three other girls, a Welsh chef with medieval face, round eyes, who followed me on my solitary walks along the cliffs, and jumped out from behind bushes. The proprietors were always having rows. She lived on drugs. He on drink. Work consisted in making beds, peeling potatoes, washing up, hoovering, and serving thirty/forty British holidaymakers lunch, tea and dinner. Being a waitress was not unlike going on the stage. I had little time for writing. The rows behind the scenes intensified, the chef threatened to leave. I collapsed one morning. I had given my notice in, but been persuaded to remain. I reached the point when a moonlight flit seemed the only way out. I arrived at the railway station in utter terror of being discovered, made to return to the hotel. I reached home speechless, dizzy, unable to bear the slightest noise. I lay in bed for days, weeks, unable to face the sun. If I went out into the garden I dug holes and lay in them weeping. I woke up in the middle of the night screaming, convinced my tears were rivers of blood, that my insides were being eaten away by an earwig that had crawled into my ear. I went to see a psychiatrist, going more from curiosity, and spent a few hours entertaining the horrified lady. I decided to climb back out of madness, the loneliness of going over the edge was worse than the absurdity of coping with day to day living.

I escaped to Paris, only to shut myself up in a room for a month. I returned to London, and found a part-time job as secretary in the painting department of an art college. I had a nice room nearby, but was turned out because my typing late at night disturbed the landlady. I moved into an attic kind of place, a small skylight, gas ring; partition next to my bed shook at night from the manoeuvrings, snores of my anonymous neighbour. I spent a winter there, writing my second book about a man called Oscar, who kills his monster child – a novel that developed into telephone directory length of very weird content, without dialogue. I finished this, rewrote it, and duly sent off to a publisher. Again rejected, but with an encouraging letter. I tried three more publishers, then gave up, put the book aside, and started another one.

My job at the art college lasted three years, and before leaving I finished the third novel, of which I did three or four versions. This was accepted. Soon after I went down with glandular TB and spent several happy months revising the book while convalescing; dreaming in fact of months, years maybe, of being in a sanatorium somewhere in the mountains, and writing masterpieces. Instead I had to face the world again, and the problems of being published. The proofs finally arrived, I couldn't open them, and spent the whole day vomiting from anxiety and depression. Eventually the galleys lay all over my room. The dream had been realized, but reading what I had written seemed like someone else's dream. A kind of involuntary commitment. And like Camus I became aware that: 'There is in me an anarchy, a frightful disorder. Creating costs me a thousand deaths, for it involves an order and my whole being rebels against order. But without it I should die scattered.'

Her head grew out from the surrounding rocks, part of the grey pock-marked structure of the shore, that was probably why he felt no surprise. The body, admittedly, might not be in harmony or in tone, a little too pink, still it could be considered a good contrast. Hair mingling with seaweed floated in a pool of pus-like water. Dark hair crawled up the wrist, stiff fingers stretched out, as though in a last attempt to grasp an insect, flatten some sea-creature, or just to cover a small area of sand for reassurance. He noted the absence of a ring.

He lit a cigarette and glanced at the cliffs, austere white knights, ready to advance. Inhaling he quickly looked down. If he moved round, his back to the sea, then his shadow fell directly upon the body, and from a certain angle it looked almost beautiful. Definitely the pink fleshiness spoilt everything. He took his coat off, and gently covered the body up. Even then the head emerging from the grey gabardine was far from satisfactory. He struggled into the coat, the lining was damp, the cigarette went out, he had no more matches. He threw the cigarette away, watching it float, drift between the strands of hair, finally, like a boat, it bobbed up and down in the same place. He picked it up and threw it towards the incoming tide. A few gulls circled above, cat-calling, one swooped and tried to peck the woman's hair, he waved the bird off, it scornfully screeched into the wind. It began raining. He brought his hat well down, and pulled his collar up, looking round for a flat piece of dry rock to sit on. He felt distracted by the body that was such a separate thing from the fine formation of the head, and he could no longer look to his shadow for assistance in the matter of improvement. He would move the body further up.

He caught hold of the woman's shoulders, cold but how soft! He dragged her across the pebbles and rocks, soon he would have her in the right position, he looked round for a suitable place. Driftwood, pieces of iron, newspaper, saturated orange peel, broken bottles, this would never do for a background. If he could only have smoked, he would have solved the problem in no time. He stared at the body, it had become patterned by pebbles, the hip-bone jutted out, that also was covered with sand and small stones; at least the crude pink had been relieved. But he would have to find an entirely different setting.

Perhaps round the cliff there would be a clear expanse of sand, clean polished pebbles, a desert compared to the jungle he was now in. He curled his fingers into the armpits, feeling the razored hair, and recalled how he had never touched anyone there. About half way he rested, sliding his hands away from the body, so that the head lolled to one side. In such a position the body alone took on a certain eye-catching quality, fish-like in the way it curved, but it was unfinished.

The cliffs from a closer quarter looked less menacing, he could see a line of damp clay at the top, an ink stain that spread, or blood, even a hair line, anything, it didn't really matter, it was there in its reality, entirety, whatever he chose to identify it with. This time he would carry the body. The rain felt like pellets of earth on his back where the body did not cover him. He heard the waves, but did not feel the spray, he tasted salt in his dry mouth, and noticed his hands were speckled with blood. As he approached the cliff that was like a piece of cake cut out against the darkening sky, the weight on his back became heavier. He stepped over the rocks, and at one time slipped, the water splashed his trousers, sliding down, though he hardly noticed.

This side was clear, except in one place where there had been a landslide. However there was plenty of sand, and the pebbles were noticeable for their scarcity. As he lowered the body he was aware of the darkness that had enveloped everything. He sank down, everything, it seemed, had been wasted. Was it really too late? He glanced round, but the rain swept over the beach, even the cliffs could not be seen. He felt for the body as a blind person would, and wiped away the sand, pebbles and seaweed; smooth flesh, though still wet, under his groping hands. He would find shelter for the night, there must be a cave somewhere. Soon he came up against the cliff, and only then realised that he had left the body behind. He was filled with overwhelming sadness, as though separated from a loved one, his mistress, wife, mother, women he had loved, or never loved. He stumbled forward and fell. He crawled the rest of the way down, feeling the sand, like insects, creep into his shoes.

The tide was nearly in, he could hear the waves lashing the rocks nearby. Where was the body, perhaps already carried out? He came to the water's edge, turned right, feeling sure he must be near it by now. In his haste, he practically tripped over the body; clasping the head he could have cried out in relief. He dragged the body across the sand, running backwards, until he felt the cliff again, here he propped the body, and began searching for shelter. At last he found a place, not exactly a cave, but adequate enough for a night. He went back quickly, the rain spat on his face, the wind swept his hat off; his hands were cold, but his head was bathed in sweat. Catching hold of the woman's hair he pulled her into a corner between a breakwater and the cliff.

The morning light so dazzled him that he had to shield his eyes before he could see anything. The tide had receded, probably now on the turn, which indicated it was well past mid-day. How had he overslept at such a time as this? However it wouldn't take long to accomplish what he had set himself. He looked the body over critically, already with the objectivity of familiarity; it wasn't all that pink, not even fleshy, apart from a slightly swollen belly, not nearly as bad as he had thought at first.

He looked across the beach, taking in, or dismissing a space here, a slight angle there, where the shadow of the cliffs fell. Several times he scoured the beach, until finally he decided to move the body about a hundred yards up, where the sand was whiter, and there were no pebbles at all. He was about to pick the body up when he heard voices nearby. Automatically he fell on top of the woman, and pressed her face close. The voices came nearer, he held his breath, pulling himself completely over the body, and felt the cold brittle lips against his own. The voices died away, only when he could no longer hear them did he roll off, lying for a time panting beside the body, his head to one side. Rubbing his lips he struggled up. A few flies settled on his neck, one crawled into the corner of his eye; he picked the body up, and marched on, it was not far to go now.

He placed the body in a horizontal position, so that the head faced the sea, then he tried it at a right-angle. In fact every position he could think of; what was wrong, the place, the body, or merely himself? He looked round the beach once more, perhaps nearer where the rocks and stones had fallen.

This time he caught hold of the woman's legs, already feeling tired, he walked slowly. Against the landslide he found the body alone spoilt the effect, it was really only the head that was needed. He searched for his pocket-knife, it was a little rusty, which meant it would take some time. He caught the woman's hair and holding the head between his legs, he started to hack. He began, after a while, to feel slightly dizzy from bending his head too low, he let go, watching the woman's head fall back upon the sand. The sun was already half way across the sky, a bright burning hole. He went on, looking almost dispassionately at his unfinished work, thinking that with the head half off the body already looked better. He wiped the knife's blade on his sleeve, and started cutting into the sinews of the neck, until the head was segregated. Triumphantly he held it up, laughing, and raised it towards the sun, as though that alone was the witness to his success. He carried the head, by the hair, into the middle of the beach, a golden patch of sand, and here he gently put it down, as he might a child, face upwards. But it refused to stay in this position, and began rolling away, until he stopped it with his foot. He picked it up, and then made a deep hole in the sand, for it to rest in. For the first time he noticed the eyes, green like sea-stones. He stepped back, it seemed too perfect, far too beautiful. The joy he had anticipated was rapidly replaced by disappointment. He began making a deeper hole, then he threw the head in, and pushed the heap of sand quickly over.

He walked back until he became aware of the headless body, the mouth slightly open, as though laughing. Now in a certain light and shade, in the corner, where he had left it, forgotten, the body looked better than it ever had before. As he approached he heard the voices again, this time much nearer. He looked at his clothes, his hands, they were covered with blood. He waded into the sea.

A DOUBLE ROOM

They had arranged to meet at 11 a.m. She arrived at 10:30. I know I must be there early or I won't go at all. Why am I going. Am I in love. No. One doesn't question. In love with the situation. Hope of love. Out of boredom. A few days by the sea. A hotel. Room overlooking sand. Gulls. Beach. Breakfast in bed. Meals served by gracious smiling waiters. But the land there is flat. Dreary. Endless. Though the sea. The sea. The whole Front to myself. But what if it rains all the time. It drizzled now as she looked out of the station. Cabs swished by. People rushed through barriers. Escape. Escape with my lover. But he isn't even that. In her small room. On her single bed they had gone so far. Fully clothed. No we'll wait it wouldn't be fair I have to leave you soon. Now the weekend he would prove to be

She clutched her bag. Glanced at the clock. And there he was. His hat cuckoo-perched on an unfinished nest. Dressed in a new suit. Mac just cleaned over his arm. Hullo love. If people stopped to look they would think we were father and daughter on our way to an aunt's funeral. They don't look. But think dirty old man. As he takes my arm. My bag.

The train. Carriages with long seats. Without divisions. Seats that make one aware of sagging shoulders. She straightened up. Straightened her skirt. Haven't seen that dress before love – new? He removed his hat. It nestled beside him. He had washed his hair. Had a bad shave. Without adding the bits of cotton wool. The train shuttled forward. Stopped. Now I could say I've changed my mind I can't go on with it I feel ill. Well how are things sweet? OK had a row with the wife oh some trivial domestic thing anyway makes it easier. Looks as if it might clear up. Brighter in the west – forecast said it would. How long does it take? About two hours love should be there in time for a beer and brunch in a nice pub somewhere. The rest of the carriage empty. Maybe someone will get in at the next stop. Pray that someone gets in. Inininininin the train chugged on over the bridge. Children threw stones into the river. He had on the green shirt. She remarked once how nice he looked in green. Matches your eyes. Eyes now stared directly at her. Was he thinking of the night. Nights ahead. Nights he had saved up for. Relishing in cosy domestic mornings. Reading the papers together. Quietly sipping tea. Quietly satisfied. Three. Four mornings ahead of them. Already I'm thinking in the third person. Seeing us as another passenger might. But no one got in at the next station. He leaned over and took her hand. She looked out of the window. Looked back at him. Cigarette? Her hand released. She dived into her bag. They lit up. He sank back. She took out a paperback. Looked at the words lumped together. Spaces between paragraphs.

The train stopped. A woman with a child got in. The child held a blue teddy bear nearly bigger than herself. They sat opposite. The woman looked across once. The child more than once. Giggling she approached. Adjusted the bear's arms. What's his name then? Tethy. He's nice isn't he? She passed the bear over. He took it and balanced it on his knees. The child started crying gimmee back gimmee gimmee Tethy gimmee. Judy come here don't disturb the gentleman there's a good girl. He smiled and handed the bear over. It growled. The child giggled and passed it over to me. Do you want to hold Tethy it's his burfday. She sucked her thumb and watched. Watching. He watched.

The houses crammed together. Back yards where men leaned on spades. Women in doorways dried their hands on aprons. Fields where boys played football. In small parks girls paused over prams. The sky strips of blue. Houses spread out. Fields. Cows. Sheep. Away from civilisation. Away from the little rituals they had been going through. Manipulated. Meetings in pubs. Fish and chips afterwards. Parties where she danced. Flirted. While he looked on. Hurried fumblings. Kisses. In a cab. Long talks by the gas fire. Holding hands in the cinema. Being shown off to his friends at dinner parties. I'm so glad he's found you he does need someone bless him and you seem so suited his wife as you probably know is

The child bounced the bear on the seat. I looked at the paperback. This autobiographical novel is a brazen confession of rebellion, trespass and blatant sexual exploitation in a world of intellectual despair and moral chaos. She closed the book. He looked up from the newspaper. His shoes highly polished. Crease in trousers nicely creased. Oh so nicely creased. Creases under his eyes. Around his mouth. Anticipation anticipation anti anti antiantiantiantiantianti. The train rattled on. The child talked to the bear. Tethy Tethy my Tethy is a naughty Tethy. The woman put away her knitting. They got out. He leaned over. It's going to be great just great love I know it will. Pressure on my knee. Only another half hour to go love. A dozen hours to come. No. Perhaps he will want to in the afternoon. An after lunch doze. I closed my eyes. Opened. More fields. More boys kicking in an orgy of mud. Men tinkered with cars. Station after station. Signals. Tunnels. Hedges. Then the sea. Flat grey. Flat washed green land on the left. Well this is it love – here I'll take your case. The hat flew on.

The wind waited round every corner. Narrow streets. Pinched faces already with the Sunday roast and glazed T.V. look. Girls. Hair in rollers. Queued in the butchers. Wondering if Jim. Fred. Or Harry will be at the dance tonight. Which pub love – what about this one looks OK doesn't it? Thin widow polished the glasses. Glass topped tables. Round. Dartboard pock-marked. Old men leaned on the bar. Looked up. Dismissed. Side-long glances. Two whiskies please. Thank you. Hungry? Mmmmmm. We'll have lunch at the hotel. Which hotel? Oh I don't know we'll find one – look around take our time I know there are at least three good ones on the Front. Looks like it's going to clear up Sir. Yes forecast said it would. Thank you Sir good day Miss.

Sky darker grey. Smell of sea. Fish. Tar. Well which hotel love – what about this one it's a three star one should be OK hope the food's good. Woman behind the register looked up. Yes we would like a double room preferably facing the sea. How long will you be staying Sir? Oh couple of days. Twin beds or double? Double please. He leaned over. Signed the book. Will you be taking lunch Sir? Yes. Lunch is served from one to two thank you Sir. Small man picked up the luggage. Struggled up three. Four flights of stairs. Doors pale yellow. Dark yellow carpet with pink flowered pattern. A door opened. His hand jingled money in his pocket. Thrust out at the appropriate time. Thank you Sir. Thank you. Door closed. Yellow wallpaper. Yellow bedspread. Pink carpet. Shiny insect-yellow dressing table. Chintz curtains. But it doesn't even overlook the sea. Ah well love it doesn't matter does it I mean

Wardrobe door creaked. Hangers. Thin wire hangers clanged. Covered by my two dresses. He's lying on the bed. Already already. I'm terribly hungry. Sighing he lurched off. Patted the eiderdown into place. My hair into place. Makeup renewed. Eyes averted. His. In the corridor past numerous yellow doors. One opened. An old man lay on the single bed. Looked up at the lamp shade. Sorry I thought it was the bathroom. Deaf. Must be deaf. Or maybe dead. A narrow bathroom. Huge Victorian bath. Pipes gurgled. The sea. A narrow dimension of winter sea from the window if pushed wide enough. Some men dragged in nets. Silently. Children screamed around them. Plug pulled. And it all came tumbling down. Down down down

Into the restaurant. Empty tables. He had chosen one near the window. Terrace. Limp bunting the wind ignored. He passed over the menu. Thin-lipped waitress stood by. Five minutes to two. Dying for her cup of tea. Feet up. Snooze. Is the dover sole nice? Yes Sir. Well we'll have that I think – sounds good doesn't it love? The waitress jabbed her notepad. Suppressed a yawn. The sea yawned out. In. Enclosed by glass. A bowl of artificial flowers. His hands spread out on his knees. What names did you sign? Mine of course love for both of us they never ask anyway. Other hotels. Other girls. Other weekends. The waitress tighter-lipped. The fish flat. Dry yellow. Little dishes with lumps of potatoes like ice cream dropped on a pavement. Vegetables as though chewed already. Looks good love doesn't it? And it is good. It will be good. I can't survive it all unless it's going to be good. It's up to me the whole thing. The next four days. Nights. I can love him. It will be all right once we've made it. Everything will be all right then. It's just this interminable waiting. Gosh you were hungry what about afters love – peach melba? No just coffee. At the corner of his mouth a piece of dover sole. I want to giggle. He folds his napkin. Well what about a little nap? I think I'll have another coffee you go on up I'll join you in a minute. The waitress peered round the door again. And again. He yawned. Smiled. Walked across and out.

Will that be all Madam? Yes thank you. Perhaps Madam wouldn't mind having her coffee in the lounge? And Madam went into the empty lounge. Heavy chintz chairs politely arranged. Politely waited. God why am I here. Well make the best of it. On the stairs the elderly bellboy stood back. Did he wink. Perhaps just a nervous tic. Which door. What number. Oh God. Smile arranged. Held. Hullo love. He pushed the newspaper aside. Red silk dressing gown. Hair on chest. She slid out of her dress. Hung it up. He had already drawn the curtains. Yellow light seeped through, She climbed over him. I love you. Her feet cold she put them between his legs. Adjusted her head. His mouth in her hair. His lips nuzzled. Came further down. She closed her eyes. Turned towards him. Take this off – here. No I'll do it. She unsnapped her brassiere. Lovely breasts you know that lovely. He held them. Held on to them. Her hand wandered over him. Clutched his hair. Legs. A little lump. Perhaps his finger. No can't be. His hands. One hand pressed her breasts. The other on her belly. Moved down. His weight moved over her. I feel the weight of my own body. Not like this oh not now not now not like this. She felt for him. How small. He slid down. Adjusted his body's length to hers. Measuring. A game of poker. Pause. Grunt. Intake of breath. Wait a minute love. Here. She took hold of him. Started rubbing. The lump became a knot. Sorry love. What is it? I don't know maybe it's because I love you so much you know frightened I won't satisfy you enough oh I don't know. Cigarette? They lay stiff. Side by side. Stared at the smoke. Ceiling. Cracked yellow. Someone padded along the corridor. Sound of rain. We need time plenty of time and we have plenty of time love – sleepy? Yes. Try and get some sleep then. She curled up under the sheet. He got up. Think I'll do a little exploring of the town get a bottle of whisky or something.

She sat up. Stared at the lamp shade. Sank down. Pulled the sheet over her head. Pushed it away. Got up. Sat in front of the mirror. Opened the drawers. Hotel headed notepaper. A few hairpins. She went out into the bathroom. Spray spattered on to the empty Front. Over the blue railings freshly painted. Half of them yet to be painted. In three months all would be a nice bright blue. The bandstand full of dapper little uniformed men who would pluck. Bang away with their brass instruments. Whether it was raining or not. Holidaymakers in paper hats. Plastic macs. Would eat ice cream. Their faces attempting to expand in a fortnight's 'away from it all'. She went back into their room. Their room that had been hundreds of other couples' scene of illicit love. After all married couples have twin beds. Well usually. At least the chambermaid wouldn't giggle with the others when changing the sheets this time. Or maybe she will. After all

After all. She took a dress down. No best to put the same one on. They'll know. They. The staff had nothing better to do than conclude. Make insinuations. As if they cared. Really. She put on the other dress and went down into the lounge. Was the rest of the hotel empty then. But no. Two women she hadn't noticed resumed talking. Huddled amongst the flowered covered chairs. A fire had been lit. She drew up a chair. Picked at a magazine. The erotic facts recorded. The most intimate characteristics of woman's sexuality. PARTIAL CONTENTS. Legend of the female organs, of the vulva, the clitoris, destruction of the hymen, circumcision of girls, the female breast, breast of Europeans, African, Asiatic women etc. Fingers dug into her bag. A young man stood in the doorway. Have you a light please? Thank you thank you very much. He took a chair. Sat behind her. He has a nice mouth. Thick hair. Rather nice smiling eyes. Is he alone. Hullo love what a lovely fire – found a good pub – well interesting – full of fishermen they've had a good day apparently good catch. Did you get the whisky? Yes it's up in our room. The young man rose. A girl in the door-way. Smiled up. He smiled down. Gosh it's damned cold out though got quite wet walking the streets – it's a nice town hasn't changed much since I came here last – like some tea love?

She poured the tea. He spread out his hands towards the fire. Shall we have it in our room we can put a little whisky in it then? He balanced the tray. It rattled as he climbed the stairs. Behind her. The elderly bellboy stood aside. Obviously hasn't a nervous tick. Wish we had a nice room facing the sea – still at least one can see it from the bathroom window. I can ask to change love. Oh no don't bother it doesn't matter really – what time's dinner? Hungry already? No just wondered. Seven I think. What shall we do? Could go to the films though I don't think there's much on. Could go to that fishermen's pub perhaps. Of course you haven't really seen the town yet – and there's a ruin too – tenth century castle I believe – it's worth seeing has dungeons and things. Is it free? No you have to pay.

They sipped tea laced with whisky. He lay on the bed. She sat on the edge. He edged her down. They kissed. A long kiss. A searching of tongues. God you do excite me love. Maybe we ought to try it with clothes on it seems that

A knock on the door. Yes? Sorry Sir just wanted to turn down the bed. Oh don't bother thank you. Just as you wish Sir – Madam. Damn maybe we should have rented a cottage after all. Stop worrying. I'm not worrying – well not really. He lit two cigarettes and handed her one. No thanks. Let him see. See see seeeeeeeeeesee. The sea whooshed down. Below. Far away. Away from the walls closing in. His face close. Closer. What's the matter love? Nothing – nothing's the matter – what time is it? She reached for his wrist. Hair crawled down and then stopped as if surprised by the sudden lumps. She leaned over. Away. Back again. And undid his shirt. She licked him. His face came up from the pillow. Oh love love love let's wait until tonight shall we – be better that way be all right then we'll have plenty of time.

They sat at the same table overlooking the terrace. Waves of whiteness curled. Uncurled. Lights along the Front hovered over circles of wetness. The middle table surrounded by young men. Laughing. Joking rugger type youths talking about rugger. The tight-lipped waitress tightly smiled. What about trying the steak this time love? Overdone medium or rare Sir? Medium I think with peas and roast. Thank you Sir. Two of the youths glanced across. Father and daughter act. But he caught hold of her hand as she helped him to some gravy. The youths glanced away. Loud laughter. I think it's stopped raining perhaps we can take a breath of fresh air afterwards love would you like that?

Along the Front. Deserted. Long sloping pavements. Carefully avoiding the puddles. She took her shoes off and ran. Laughing. On to the beach. Down to the water's edge. She heard him panting. Crunching over the pebbles. Her hair over her eyes. She did not sweep away. Lights of the town distant. The sky uplifted from the heaving mass of darkness. That was the sea. Sound of sea. Sounds of other seas. Other days. Spent in other places. Under foreign skies. But I can't afford to indulge. It's not fair fair fair fairee fairee fairee. Gulls swooped out of the folds of darkness. Tips of white unfolded into expanse of whiteness. Above her. She laughed into the wind. With the wind. Her face tilted towards his. Make love to me make love make love to meeeeee. Ah love what here it's so damned cold. He embraced her. She shook against him. Shook with uncontrollable laughter. He gently lifted her face up. We will tonight love or if not then tomorrow eh we have a few days yet. I'm cold let's go back – or go and have a drink.

They went into the public bar. Men looked up. Paused in laughter. Shall we try the saloon love? No let's go back to the hotel. They passed a large hotel that looked closed. But waiters gazed out of long windows. Maybe we should have gone there better food perhaps. Oh I don't know looks pretty grim to me. But at least the rooms all face the sea love.

They went into the hotel bar. The youths roared. Raring to get high. Or already high. Slapped each other on the back. We have got that whisky in our room shall we go up love? They sat on the edge of the bed. Drank from the tooth glasses. Until the bottle was nearly empty. Well I'm turning in love. But it's only nine o' clock. Oh well we can get up early – might be a nice day.

She shook out her nightdress. Went into the bathroom. Sat on the toilet and waited for the bath to fill. Water lukewarm. Someone rattled the handle. She stopped singing. Love can I come in? Shivering she reached for the latch. Thought you might like your back scratched. Mmmmmmmm. He pulled his shirt sleeves up and knelt. Applied soap over his hands. Wrists. Have you locked the door? Yes love. He applied his hands over her. Breasts. Belly. What about my back? Just a sec. Oh it's cold. Here. He held the towel out. Giggling she wrapped it round herself. Here I'll dry you. He rubbed her body. Knelt and kissed her toes. She wriggled. Love love love oh dear love. You better go first or else someone will see us. Oh what the hell. Well you better. She locked the door. Sat on the toilet. Opened the towel and looked at herself. I'm not in love and that's all there is to it. She pulled the plug. Notinlovenotinlovenotin. The pipes. Behind walls. Water rushed out. Into the sea.

He lay on the bed. Smoking. Green striped pyjamas. Still smelling of detergent. His wife had ironed. She slid down beside him. He switched the light off. I'd rather have it on sweet. He switched the light on. His hand. Hands. She flung off her nightdress. Bent over him. His breathing quickened. She caught her breath and took him in her mouth. Like a little boy's. But gradually

She spread her legs out and felt for him again with her hands. Kiss me kiss me there. He obeyed. She held his head. Held on to his head. Hair. Closed her eyes. Held her breath. And froze. She watched herself. Her body. Her lumps of flesh solidified. Love love what is it – what's happened are you all right? She opened her mouth. The scream couldn't. Wouldn't. Be forced out. It lay. Struggled. Thumped within the blood cells. Ribs. That closed in on the scream. That became separated. Someone else's scream. The child. The girl. The virgin. The woman. Until they joined forces. Screamed at the person outside who refused to collaborate. She felt him lift her from him. Gently put the sheet. Blankets over her shoulders. Let's try and sleep shall we – we're both tired and had too much to drink and in the morning it'll be all right. She felt his back against her back. She waited. Stared into the dark. Was he staring into that too? But no. He was already asleep. Snoring. Little grunts at first. God I hope he's not the whistling kind. The snores grew louder. She sat up. Reached for a cigarette. What is it love – can't you sleep? No. Maybe if you… I can't sleep if you snore can I. Was I – sorry you should give me a nudge. She jabbed out the cigarette. Turned over. And waited. The snores came as before. Yet not as before had been. Heavier. Insistent. Demanding. She nudged him. He grunted and rolled over on to his back. She closed her eyes. Put the pillow half over her head. The snoring continued. Grew louder. The whole room vibrated. She hurled herself up. Was I snoring again? Yes. Oh God – look I'll sleep over there in the chair. He took the eiderdown off. The pillow. And huddled into the chair. You can't sleep there can you sweet? Well what else can we do? I don't know – wish you'd brought your ear plugs – wish I even had some sleeping pills. She watched the dot of his cigarette move upwards. Down. It's really quite comfortable love it's better this way. She moved over to the warmth where his body had been. And waited. The snores came. Every minute. I could time them like a woman in labour. Less than a minute. She got up and went out.

She leaned her head out of the bathroom window. The rain made her face wetter. The scream moved up into the lump. A fist thrust in her throat. Spread out. The scream emerged in a coughing bout. I'll leave tomorrow. Catch the first train back. Go and pack now. Wait at the station. Maybe there's a late train. She sat on the toilet. Shivered. What a situation to find myself in. No one to blame except myself. The handle rattled. Are you all right love? Yes yes. I could try and sleep in here but then someone will want to use the damned place. She opened the window wider. Lines of white broke up the shore. Waves of blackness swallowed up the houses. I'm so cold so cold. She opened the door but closed it as someone came along the corridor. She waited for silence. She tried again and ran into the room. He smoked. Hunched in the chair. We should have got separate rooms. Perhaps tomorrow we can go to another hotel. No I'm going back. Oh my dear…

She buried herself in the bed. Against the wall. I'll wait until you're asleep first love. She heard the lighter click. Shut. Pause. Sound of doors. Opened. Closed. The lighter clicked. She waited. Waited for the next click. And the first faint light to edge in through the curtains. Soon the light came. A thin light that brought the relief of shadows. She could see him. Heard him turn. Confined to eiderdown. Chair. She closed her eyes. When she opened them the room was speckled with light. He was shaving. Did you get any sleep love? A bit what about you? Not really. His face paper yellow. Pink eyes. He grinned. At least it's not raining – in fact it's a gorgeous day and we'll go and have a look at that castle unless of course you are going back? I don't know just don't know we can't obviously go on like this can we? Oh my dear love love love – come on let's have a good breakfast and then go out shall we?

She decided she really didn't want any breakfast. Just a cup of tea. So he went down alone. She dressed slowly. Glanced in the mirror. What a sight. But what did it matter. She had decided. The scene had already been set long before they ever came here.

They met in the foyer and walked out along the Front. On to the pier. In silence. Watched the men fling their fishing lines in. A few fish struggled. Thumped around on the iron grilles. Gave a final twitch then slid down with the others in the basket.

The castle surrounded by a moat of dryness. The guide asked if they wanted to be shown around. They walked round together. The guide went back to sleep. Round walls with scaffolding. Crumbling walls. Walls that were no longer walls. Large rooms with wooden floors. Jewellery and fossils under glass. Please Do Not Touch notices everywhere. Smell of must. Please Do Not Smoke round every corner. Endless passage that was not so endless. The castle was round. A dungeon she quietly went into while he looked up at a sword. She heard him go past. She shrank into the darker corner of the cell. His footsteps grew fainter. Above her. She looked through the narrow bars. At the triangle patch of grass. Please

Do Not Throw Litter Here. Please Keep Off The Grass. She saw him standing on the fortress. He leaned against a cannon. His hand thrust upwards. Shielded his eyes. He must be looking out to sea. She heard his footsteps approach. She stifled a giggle. And walked out. Oh there you are were you hiding? No I wondered where you were. Well we've seen just about everything I think. What about the other dungeons? OK. They walked again the narrow passage. Where no sun had entered. God what a place I could imagine a murder here – in fact you could well... She sprang back. Her mouth open. Closed into a closed smile as his hands came out. Oh don't frighten me like that. Stupid – God your imagination love. All the same it is frightening. And she sprang from the wall. Ran past him. Laughing. Screaming out. You won't catch me never ever never. She heard her voice bounce back. And his laughter. His gasps. Until he had caught her up. They held hands. Crossed the drawbridge. Thanked the guide who gave them a pamphlet history of the castle. Who went back to sleep behind his desk.

They went into a seafront cafe and ordered coffee. Lovely day Sir – Miss. A group of girls entered and went over to the juke box. Hypnotised by the choice. Oh there's nothing here not even the Rolling Stones. They sat down. Nudged each other. Giggled. I have to go back. Oh love. Well. They stared into their cups. He looked up. Across. She looked down. His shoes were covered in seaweed. Sand. She nodded. Give it a day just another day love I mean we've hardly been here and

47

They walked through streets. Past houses that never varied with their lace curtains. Back gardens. Shrubberies. Back yards with washing. Parts of bicycles. Spare parts of cars. Boys in fields played football. Curtained windows. People still in bed. Or yawned over newspapers. Or watched the television.

In the restaurant their table was occupied by the young couple. The middle table surrounded by women. Middle aged with hats. Hats with feathers. Without feathers. Bits of veil. One woman stood up to give a speech, They all clapped. The young couple leaned towards each other. Their plates full of unfinished food.

The afternoon came. Went. And the night. Repetitive of the night before. Yet not quite. They got drunk. But didn't attempt to make love. Attempted to sleep. And the morning faced their faces now white. They walked by the sea. She finally said they would go could go back together. They went for a final drink in the large hotel. Sat encased by glass and aspidistras. Without talking. If accidentally they touched they apologised. Looked at each other when the other wasn't looking. The sky expanded in blueness. Their mouths sucked in as the plants sucked in the water the waiter sprayed from a plastic watering can.

They packed their things. She waited outside. Watched him pay the bill. Smile at the woman behind the desk. The elderly bellboy brought out the luggage. Winked with both eyes. Had a good time Miss – glad the weather cleared up for you – come back again won't you – taxi

Sir? No thanks we'll walk. They walked up the street. Away from the sea. Past the pub with the glass topped tables. Shall we have a drink? Have one at the station I think love if there's time. The bar closed. They sat in the buffet and had a cup of tea. Lukewarm. The train roared in. The carriages separated by glass doors. A corridor. They went into an empty carriage. Hope no one gets in. So do I. He brought out half a bottle of whisky and opened it. Passed over. She took a tiny sip then a longer one and handed it back. The train moved out. Wheels clanked along. Past the sun-splashed sea. Pale green slice of land that spread out into deeper green. The deeper blue. I'm sorry love really I am. So am I. But I can see you – I mean we will still see each other after we get back? I think not I mean it is impossible isn't it you can see that. At each station they looked out. No one got in. Or if they did they looked once into the carriage then passed on along the corridor. She leaned over. Held his hand. Pressed. He sighed. I hate it to end like this but

The fields. Hedges vanished. Suburbs crawled in and out. The football fields now dry. Now empty. The river red flecked with white. The power station powered out its smoke. They walked through the barrier. Paused in the half empty station. Well. Well? Well I'll 'phone you. No it won't be any use will it? Well then it's goodbye – goodbye love. And he rushed into the underground. She caught a bus back. Asked the conductor for change. Climbed the stairs to her room. And lay on the bed. The telephone rang. She opened the door quietly. Heard someone talk.

She took out a cigarette. Put it back. And collapsed on the bed. Got up and searched for the change. Went down on to the second floor and put the money in the box. His voice. As though he had a cold. She heard her own. That was not her own. Voice. Look let's meet up some time this week and talk about it. When? Thursday? What about tomorrow? Tonight? OK I'll come round? Yes – see you later then. She put the receiver carefully down. Went up to her room and unpacked. Washed her face and applied makeup. The face she saw was smiling little smiles that broke into a wide grin.

EVERY CRIPPLE HAS HIS
OWN WAY OF WALKING

The house was old. They were older. The sisters. They celebrated Queen Victoria's Jubilee. Cried at her funeral. At least if they hadn't actually seen these events they witnessed it all in the newspapers. The house full of newspapers. Paper bags within paper bags. Letters. Photographs. Pieces of brocade. Satin. Ribbons. Lockets. Hair. Broken spectacles. Medicine bottles. Empty. Foreign coins. Trunks. Cases. Cake. Biscuit tins. And mice. The child never knew whether it was the mice or one of her aunts wheezing in the long nights. Or maybe just the wind from the sea. The downs. Whistling in the chimney. Other nights she knew it was Aunt Molly battling with her asthma. Or Aunt Sally sucking tea from a saucer. And the bed creaked in the room below. As grandma turned over. Back again. From the waist up. Did she have legs? The child thought of them. Thought she saw them like sticks under the sheet. About to thrust up. With barnacles and millions of half-dead fish clinging. The old woman's flesh. Scaly. Her eyes like someone just risen from the ocean bed. But then she was grandma.

And all grandmothers must look like that. Confined to an enormous bed. Yet not so enormous. For she filled all parts. At all times. As she filled the house with her demands. Commands. In her little girl's voice. When not eating. Not sleeping. Whined for the bedpan. Another cup of tea. And if Aunt Sally stopped making kitchen noises then she whined for the bedpan again and accused her younger sister of indulging in forty winks. For the house belonged to grandma. Every item down to the shrimp pink corset and purple dress Aunt Sally wore had been billed to grandma. She after all had married. And no one now would point out she had stolen Aunt Molly's intended. That a long time ago. And he who had made the mistake by proposing in a letter from India to the wrong sister had long since departed. They lived as best. The three. In the worst. Through thick and thin. They lived their roles. Respected. Detested. Each other's virtues. Little vices. Whims. And waited for the day the child's father would pay a visit. That day would surely be tomorrow. If not tomorrow then the next day. When Nicholas Montague. Monty to them all. Would tread the path. Into the house. Receive their love. And tell them of his travels. Successes. Though Aunt Molly would look past him. As if she recognised in his shadow some remembered dream. Go on sorting out little bundles of letters. Comb her long white hair. Thin. So thin it was more of a veil covering her head. Face of crushed carnation that sprouted from the black bent root of velvet. The child would look past him too. Perhaps. At the portrait. For comparison. While Aunt Sally clucked round him. Teeth clicking. Little bird eyes upon the nephew who could do no wrong. If he did a wrong in others' eyes then he did it because there was no alternative.

The days grew into each and out of each night. With the habits. Dreams. Tales of days gone by. The horse-drawn buses. Dinner. Tennis parties. Musical evenings. Picnic outings with cousins by the Thames. Sunday strolls in Kew Gardens. And the Crystal Palace. For the child these stories merged with those of The Goose Girl. The Snow Queen. And Cinderella. Each of these she was. Saw her aunts as grown ancient but with a wave of the magic wand they would change into beautiful queens with quick queenly steps. She felt sure her father would have this wand. Transform the old castle on the hill. The old ladies. Herself. Into a magical world where they would all live together happily ever after.

Weeks. Months. Years. Came. Went. After hours of anticipation. The child saw the calendar only in the mirror. She was still not taller than Aunt Sally. She thought the day would never come when she would be. Though she forgot this problem when she didn't have to bend to peer through the keyhole at Aunt Molly. Whole mornings spent on the landing. Watching her aunt go through the never-changing rituals. Always the child hoped that some morning. Some time the white-haired apparition would do something different. Or maybe not do anything at all. Lie motionless in her black velvet. This the child hoped for more than anything. The door then would surely magically open. The room at last hers to explore. There were the corners. Dimensions. She never saw from her one-eyed viewing. Then there were the cupboards. Drawers. These must be filled with all kinds of mysterious things. Boxes her aunt bent over. But never brought out whatever lay there. Her hands shook. Hovered over something. Then the lid closed and her aunt locked the box. Held the box. Nursed it in her lap. Her lips moved. Drawn in. The child tiptoed away along the landing where the wind mocked the carpet. Played with the carpet on the stairs. Down into the kitchen the child crept to make Aunt Sally jump in the larder. Oh you wicked child you'll be the death of me yet here take this into your grandma her tongue's hanging out for a cup of tea quick now and I'll give you a piece of bread and butter pudding.

The child took the tray. Tried not to spill the tea into the saucer. If she did before reaching grandma's door then the lions would eat her up. But they were preferable to the lioness with the little lion's growl that greeted her offering. So there you are well bring it over here that's right now care – ach child you're so clumsy and what's your Aunt Sally doing taking another nap I suppose well don't stand there child like an imbecile just like your…

Her mouth filled with cake. Tea. Denture coping. Body manoeuvres. Just her eyes. Waterlogged. Stared at the child. Her head moved in time to the munching. Sipping. Swallowing. Plump ringed fingers filled the space between eiderdown. The small hole that presumed to be a mouth. The child held her breath against the smells. Urine. Stale food. And medicines. She counted the flies on the limp strips of sticky yellow near the curtained windows. Listened to cupboards. Drawers being opened. Closed. In the room upstairs. Unable to hold her breath any longer she rushed out. From grandma's munching. Grinding. Into the kitchen where Aunt Sally hardly bent over the oven. Drew the baking tin out. Blinked in the warmth. Her own warm approval. Pleasure. Ah it looks a good one this time. She tested with a knife. The two of them bent over this treasure of golden brown. With little smiles. Hands of assurance. They ate. Hardly two mouthfuls when the child begged her aunt to sing. Sing anything. But you know all I know is Little Brown Jug. Well sing that then. The child clapped her hands. Licked the sticky remains from around her mouth. And felt even the wind under the back door sounded friendly now. Plants in the outhouse nodded in their full row of participation. Clouds danced lightly on the brow of the hill. Poppies and blue flowers bowed in acknowledgement towards the house. And the child knew if the sea was nearer that too would chuckle in the warm conspiracy. Sing sing Auntie and do that little dance you do. Ah you little devil I haven't got all day to play with you get along with you now go and play in the garden. The child laughed. Made to hug her aunt. Made all kinds of promises. Pretended to cry. Tickled her. Until the demanded song burst out and her aunt skipped one. Two. Three oops there now you'll be the death of me oh my oh dear little brown jug don't I love theeeee there I'm worn out and there's your grandma calling. Off she went muttering. Dress dusted the floor. Caught in the door as she wiped the tail ends of pudding from the corners of her moustached upper lip.

The child amused herself in the garden. Mud pies. Went in search of the tortoise. Poked sticks in mole hills. Lifted stones from the path. Watched the ants go this way and that. Some took cover under her shoes. When she pressed down. Stared for a long time at the little red stains on the stonework. The house stared back. With heavy-lidded eyes. She looked up and thought she saw the sea had rolled itself into the sky. Then down. She saw Aunt Molly draw back from the window. Hands that came from the dark space behind. On their own. Drew the curtains closer together.

She raced with the wind round the house. Jumped over the path. Crawled through the long grass. Weeds. Startled a blackbird that was after her nose. The army of wallflowers shook with astonishment. Behind them the overgrown hedge held strange shapes. Shadows fell out. Crawled towards the child. Knocked on the windows. At night. Noises of the dark joined the nightly noises of those who inhabited the house. And those who didn't. If only she had wings she could fly away from them all. And then.

Well then she could search for the one who would be sure to wave them all away with his wand. Flapping her arms she ran screaming into the house. Up and down the stairs. Two. Three. At a time. The wind joined in. Grandma collaborated. Until the house screamed its way out of the day.

The night noises entered. Tomorrow I think he's coming I can feel it I can sense it. Who's coming Auntie? Why your father of course. And Aunt Sally's eyes rolled away. Back. Towards her flushed nose. What's he like? He's a good man and he's your father yes Monty is…

The child turned away from her aunt's mutterings. From the glazed eyes that would soon be dabbed with a handkerchief smelling of mothballs or the sleeve of her purple dress. She crept up to the landing. For her last goodnight spying on Aunt Molly. Who dipped fingers into her dinner. Surrounded by her boxes. Letters. Coughing. Her whole body heaved as she stretched up. Bent over. As though attacked by some unseen spirit. Strange noises came through the keyhole. Came from her aunt's open mouth. The child turned into the noise of the wind that attacked all sides of the house. All corners. Gaps. Cracks. In doors. Windows. Struggled with something. Someone. Way up in the loft where the hotwater tank hissed. Where the mice waited. In her own room the child rearranged dolls. Told them tales of the magician they would see tomorrow.

Tomorrow came as yesterday. And the next day. With the wind. Rain. The child stayed in the house. Listened to what the wind told to the walls. And then again to what the walls told. Showed. What was shown when a door flew open. When closed. At times the house had secrets the child found were not revealed to her. When the place wrapped itself up. As if wounded. Like an animal refusing to show itself. At such times the child curled up with a favourite toy and tried to sleep. Often she did sleep. Feeling that if she ignored everything then they would emerge. Give their secrets to her once again.

Such an afternoon when she woke up. Heard laughter. Strange tinkling laughter as though the house had suddenly filled with young girls. She ran downstairs. The laughter came from Grandma's room. She peered in. Aunt Sally sat on the end of the bed. Legs swinging as if she were on a swing. Her face expanded in smiles. She nodded over a piece of paper. Well well he's really coming tomorrow oh my goodness oh dear. About time too. The child heard her grandma grunt then whisper. Saw her aunt frown. Of course he will after all she's his child there's no denying that and my goodness how surprised he'll be to find what a big girl she is now. Well see she's dressed properly the way she goes around why it's a scandal a proper little tomboy and see she washes behind the ears tonight Sally. Yes yes oh my goodness he's really coming Monty's really coming I must make a nice bread pudding perhaps we should get a little wine in I mean just oh well I have a little port left I think Monty likes port just a little port. Her words lost somewhere in the small piece of paper she brought up. Adjusted her glasses. Nodding. Lips moved. While the bed creaked under her. Oh Sally for heaven's sake you've read that at least half a dozen times you must know it off by heart now go and make some tea I'm dying for a nice cup of tea and don't forget to ring Goodmans order a chicken Monty likes chicken I remember as a little boy he…

The child went quietly into the lounge. And looked at the portrait. Bent closer. She whispered. In front of the grand piano she put her wet thumb on a black note. Held there. Put all her fingers on black and white. Leaned over and watched the insects with white fuzzy heads rise to greet her. Up. Down. Until her aunt trotted in. Shouted stop that your grandma's trying to sleep and you know you mustn't touch the piano Monty will – your father doesn't like his piano touched by anyone except himself and he's coming tomorrow we've had a telegram yes Monty will…

The child swung round on the stool. Kicked up her legs. Will he bring me a present? Perhaps perhaps but he's bringing himself and that's enough now upstairs with you it's late.

In the dark. In bed. The child thought she heard the laughter again. Thought she heard steps on the path. She leaned out of the window and watched the gate swing. The shadows swung out. The shape on the hook attached to the door grew a monstrous head. But tomorrow everything would be all right.

They waited all day. Waited in retreats. Pursuits. Tidying rooms. Dusting the piano. Baking. Cups of tea breaks. Grandma shrieked every half-hour. Aunt Molly continued as all the days before. Combed out her hair. Plucked the strands from her dress. Rustled amongst paper. Boxes. And had two attacks between meals. The child hid behind the hedge. Watched every bus. Every car. Until the wind. Rain. Swept her back into the house. Well maybe he's had an unexpected engagement held up in the traffic caught the flu. Aunt Sally muttered. Grandma screamed from the bedpan. Where's Monty then what could have happened? The child sat in front of the portrait. Stared into eyes she had been told were velvet brown. She saw them as black as Aunt Molly's dress with flecks of white he might pluck out in moments. And the wand? Well even if he didn't appear to have one he would have it hidden up his sleeve and she alone would know his secret.

She heard a car drive up. Stop. She ran to the window and saw a man step out. Down the path. She thought she saw a woman sitting in the car. She hid behind the curtain. Heard Aunt Sally shout. Her feet tapped from the kitchen to the front door. Monty oh Monty how lovely to see you we thought you…

Then his voice. Rising. Falling. The child wrapped the curtain round herself. She heard the steps. The heavier tread behind the tapping go into grandma's room. Grandma's little voice that seemed to be quieter. Almost a gurgle. The door closed. She waited. Heard the grandfather clock strike in the hall. And knew she had missed the cuckoo clock upstairs. Perhaps…

But the door opened. Again she heard the heavy tread. Her aunt's voice high pitched. The man's low. Rising. Falling. In a lowness that seemed linked to the wind coming off the sea. Well where is she Sally? I just don't know Monty where the child's gone perhaps she's in the garden playing I'll go and see. The child held her breath as she heard the tread fall into the room. Saw a shadow on the wall opposite. That moved across. Vanished. She peered round and saw the man stood near the piano. Heard her aunt call. Calling. Saw her on the garden path. Turn and enter the house. Well Monty I don't know where she could have got to I expect she'll be around soon are you hungry Monty I've got the dinner on some nice chicken andhowlongareyou…

But he silenced her by playing the piano. The child watched him. Watched her aunt quietly take a chair and sit down. He played and hummed. Then as suddenly as he began. Stopped. Well Sally I won't be staying too long. Oh Monty we thought… Well you see I have a concert tomorrow and I must get back tonight – just a short visit I'm afraid just to see how you all are and also pick up a few things I need this piano will be collected tomorrow also those chairs by the way what's Molly got in her room I've forgotten hasn't she that ivory table and how's her asthma these days of course she's getting on now has she made her will Sally you must make sure she does that I'm certain she's got quite a little gold mine up there no one knows about eh? Yes yes Monty but I'm sorry you won't be staying long – are you – I mean are you in need of – I've saved up a little for you Monty I know things get difficult for you and well…

The child moved. Made towards the door. Ah there you are been hiding all this time from your father then come here darling my Sally hasn't she grown come on then don't be frightened of your own father. He moved towards her. Arms outstretched. She looked at his feet. Her own. Felt his arms enclose her. Pick her up. Swing her round. She closed her eyes. When she opened them she saw their faces below. The walls spun. Collided. She leaned away from the man whose lap she sat in. Felt his hands on her head. His body pressed against hers. Smelling of tobacco. And something else she wasn't sure about. But she felt sure he didn't have the wand up his sleeve. Or anywhere. He hugged her. Hugged the breath from her. My little girl my she's quite a big girl now eh is she a good girl and is she behaving herself Sally? She saw her aunt smile. Nod. Head tilted. Little bird eyes raised towards the man who held on. Grasped. Fondled. Clutched. The child struggled. Fell away from the arms. She stood back. Looked at the portrait.

Looked at the man who grinned down at her. His arms now limp. Hung over the leather chair arms. One hand came up. Burrowed in his pocket. Then out. He held a bright coin between finger and thumb. Look a present for you darling buy some sweeties with or something eh there's a good girl. The child wondered if this coin had come out of her aunt's little box she knew Aunt Sally kept these round shiny coins in a box maybe he did too. She went forward. And again came into contact with his arms. Legs. Covered in tweed. Tobacco smelling.

And the other smell. Like the bottle grandma dabbed herself with. Only stronger. Much sweeter. She took the coin. Pressed the warmth into her own warmth. While the man jogged her up and down on his knees.

Later she felt his knee under the table. After the meal he picked her up. Kissed her. Said he would come up later and tuck her up.

She waited. The light on. Listened to the voices way down below. Until the wind rose. She heard only that caught in the chimney. She crept out. Down the stairs. And leaned against the door. Grandma's voice wailed. Aunt Sally seemed to be crying. The third voice mumbled. The child looked through the keyhole but saw only a hand clutching a pipe. Soon not even that. She curled her toes and watched the rug lift up and down in front of the kitchen door. Until movement in the room made her run into the kitchen. Into the larder. The voices everywhere. Coming from all corners of the house. Even the wind had fled. The heavy thud of doors. Heavier tread in. Out of rooms. Lights switched on. Off. On in the kitchen. She saw her aunt empty the little box. Count the bright coins out on the table. Saw her pick them up and patter out shouting Monty Monty here before you go just a little something to tide you over for a few days. The child crouched. Breathed in the cake smells. Biscuits and candles. Smelt her own hands that had the smell of tobacco like the damp earth that lingered after her games in the garden. She heard the front door open. Close. The house was silent. She crept out. Ran up to the landing. Aunt Molly stood at the window. Half behind the curtain. She seemed to be chuckling. Hair in one long plait ended in a pink bow in the small of her back that swung from side to side.

The child ran into her own room. Looked out of the window but saw only the gate swinging slightly. She jumped into bed. Threw the bedcover over her head. She heard Aunt Sally mount the stairs. Grandma's voice shrieked Sally Sally when did Monty say he'd be coming again? Her aunt paused. Breathed heavily. Oh Monty will be here again soon don't worry go to sleep now yes he'll be back and maybe he'll stay a bit longer have some bread pudding next time.

The child turned over and listened. Listened until the walls. Doors. Breathed in quietness. In the dark. She gave her secret to the house.

Yeah maybe I ought to get organised, trouble is I don't know what I really want to do. OK so I could earn five thousand a year, but I'm not ending up like those other slick ad chaps. Christ they're so mass-consumed they can't even shit straight. And the exhibitions these other jerks have they're for the birds, so provincial. I want to do something no one else has ever done as good, if only to drive a van better than anyone before, thought of motor racing once, well maybe I'll end up growing cabbages. Take my grandfather, he potters about the farm, all these years doing shit all, apart from watering a few plants, that's why he's lived so long. Man of ideas though, bought two trawlers for herring fishing, made anchovy paste, sold for miles around, yeah he's really wild. It's great out on the West Coast, ninety miles of black sand, tufts of grass, you know, surf and spray; turf like a golf course all over, yeah man it's space alright. Only other place as good as where the Abos live, wouldn't mind a life with them, rest of Australia like a dust bowl. They ought to shift the other zombies to New Zealand, only way to save the situation now. Yeah perhaps I am a Commie, I don't dig Marx though, at least I'm not a Nationalist Fascist, and all that jazz, but I rather like the idea of sharing. Get a few people working for me, I produce the ideas, they perform, why not, yeah like this guy Michelangelo. Like the other night I got sloshed, brought back some chap, we did a painting together, that's the real stuff, let it out first go, leave it at that, all these other crappy painters, they would be better if they used their pricks. Not that I dig this pop art, they haven't anything to say. Now Mailer could do anything and get away with it; I suppose you've got to be a genius, or something, to do that, otherwise it's sheer hard work. I worked myself sick once, didn't want to see anyone, locked myself in my room, but this beat guy, man is he a real beat beat, didn't care an arse hole for anyone, get pissed up, sleep on the floor, or in a chair in his clothes. Well this guy climbed out on to my window sill, and squatted there reading poetry to me all day long, till I let him in and we went to bed together. No I'm not queer, OK so I've fucked a few fellows, but I'm not gay. Yeah I know that place, some smart blonde chap tried seducing me, I was so innocent in those days, shit if I went there now, yeah maybe I ought to try everything, who knows. This club in New York we all went to, they stood around just staring, some in drag, quiet music and all that crap in the background, sure I've thought about it; maybe I ought to sleep with some guy. Told myself lately I don't need sex any more, gone so hip I don't think I do now. Wish I hadn't had so many women, like a machine in the end.

This chick I lived with, just a convenience, screwed her every night, again in the morning, get up at eleven and know she had cooked some breakfast, Jesus it gets so boring. She was a nymphomaniac, that was her trouble. I want it to mean something, not just sex. All these chicks dote on one, that's why I've given them up. Now take these crazy negros in their white sneakers, paisley ties, two vents in their jackets and all that crap, not really wild, just conservatively wild you know, watch how they treat their chicks. One in the subway went up to this broad and said Get in there I'm going to fuck you, she did too, right there and then in the tube, isn't that great, I mean it's real, that's how a movie should be made. Like I was walking down this street with a camera, I mean these are real, matches, sugar lumps, like this friend who's making a movie about some kid wanting a pair of roller skates so she walks a big poodle. It's all shit otherwise, look at this jerk, fourth Earl of Onslow gets a Maori whare over here, what right has he to do that, I feel like taking it straight back, what good will it do here?

OK so this hip business is all a façade, underneath I'm just a shy regular guy, but man it takes a long time to forget a bourgeois background such as mine was, and right now I'm in the middle of a change. So I'm not going to this party, only be like the rest, petty provincial, lots of grog maybe, and chicks' tits to pull, what a drag, they're so square. Take that chick, why when he's gone I bet she'll be fucked madly by the night watchman. London makes me shit, it's not even a city, whole of England is composed of Londons. What slobs cutting down trees like that, they really are sick, and that glass on top, who would want to climb over their crappy wall anyway? Jesus I'm getting out.

UNTITLED
(NEH MAN IT'S LIKE THIS)

Neh man it's like this I'm through with image, it's the word now, reality that's what I want. Take this guy with six others leaving the Bronx, cops were waiting for them, so he shot one down, just like that, man it's real, none of this stuff these slobs care about. Look at that cat in his crappy outback outfit, what a slob. What do you think they're thinking? Whether or not he'll make it with her, and she's wishing she could make it with the guy two yards away. Made it with a gorgeous nymphomaniac negress, man she was wild, crazy, in full view of the whole of New York, with the light on, man across the way cleaning his teeth, having an orgasm. OK Henry Miller. Analysing me on every withdrawal, on the floor, in the sink, she was wild. And all those pretty boys, sure it's easy to go queer over there. No he's not, sure he's slept around with men, that doesn't make him camp though. Anyway makes a change doesn't it? Called round at 2 a.m. to say goodbye before going to Paris, guess he was in love with me at one time. Went round together in New York, until he shacked up with this guy. Yeh we went blonde together, dyed it overnight at some party so they told me. This crazy negro got into my bed, naked, slithering like a fish on a marble slab. Yeh I guess I almost went queer, didn't want it get too involved. These slobs over here, they might look camp, but that's as far as it goes, they don't know how to swing man. Now take B and I, we do things together, we just swing man, doesn't matter what it's like, who signs it, all the same, what the hell, we paint together, he's great, real wild. What I mean is they don't know how to string a film together, now this guy in L.A. well he made a film about this little girl taking out her poodle in the park every morning, as big as a horse, well isn't that great, I mean there she was with this dog, bigger than she was, but it wasn't even a horse. Yeh I want to write, words mean more. Take the other night, out in the street, I was sliding in dog's shit, and B. shouts Come on Man stop crapping about, isn't that great, don't you think I can write about that, I mean there I was in all that crap and he says stop crapping. That's how it should be. Sure dreams come into it, but it's got to be real, like that film of the girl with her poodle. Yeh it's an idea, sure it's an idea, but I would have a dog fucking the woman's body on the beach, while the man runs into the sea without clothes, it's wild though, really wild. Like this negress, she was an opera singer, we swung so high, man was I crazy about her, I left my balls behind me, in Madison Avenue. Say we're not hip this way are we? Take all these slobs, in a club sucking a whisky bottle like it was a dummy, shit, they're all sick. They always want to come back too, can't understand it, come back to England and the Queen, who wants to live in such a crappy place? Now if I went to Cornwall, I guess I'd get to think, man this is it, this is great, and just go on sticking there, in the same old rut. Take this writer chap I know, got married to a Maori girl, lives in the Bush, how does he exist? Sydney's the place, yeh man, in a year's time, that'll be it. Sure I'll work tomorrow, for twenty-four hours after taking a pill, yeh you can get 'em on a doctor's prescription, just go on working, getting high at the same time. I can't give you one, last time I couldn't get rid of this girl, man was she a sticker, stayed with me for a week, and the other night at some party she came up and slapped me, slapped me down, I was so pissed. Yeh maybe I'll go back to New Zealand, volcano erupted the other week, almost forgotten about volcanos erupting. House on the beach, swim over to some islands climb the rocks, go water skiing, maybe get eaten by an octopus, barbecues at night, yeh maybe I'll go over for a couple of months, then come back here.

LIVING IN THE PRESENT
(WITH ROBERT SWARD)

THE LUFTWAFFE TRADITION OF ALLEGORICAL FANTASY

As Mr. Harvey Matusow, a lying informer the Nazi leaders so derelict recanted in his *False Witness*, this question Telford Taylor has been unable entirely to resolve, wealth and publicity were major motives, a most useful compendium; and to these Dr. Zeligs has added psychological disorder The Fuehrer was seeking not to destroy Great Britain, but to compel her and of the recollections of those acquaintances who would speak, the German reign in Europe. On Hiss, the psychoanalysis is highly impressive Goering had promised that the Luftwaffe tradition of allegorical fantasy follows the straightforward saga pattern. And goes far to explain much that has remained bewildering. The decision raised more problems than it solved.

WHEN SQUEEZED OR STEPPED ON THEY EXPLODE

When he had opened the second seal several hundred servicemen were ordered into the area and there went out another horse that was red: the bomblets an Airforce spokesman and he that sat on him would not elaborate. A civilian official said the accident was caused and there went out another horse that was red. Military spokesman said the explosion would be painful and that they should kill one another. The brownish disks. He did not explain. Power was given. I heard a voice in the midst of the four beasts, the secret device being developed for use. Donald Spinelli of Fort Walton Beach found one. And when he had opened the fourth seal, Choctawatchee Bay along the Florida Pan handled, and his name that sat on him was Death, and Hell followed. Mr. Spinelli, 24, was treated. Governor Tiemann manned a pitchfork. The Governor was joined by University of Nebraska College of Agriculture Dean E. F. Frolik. Both had performed. And they sung a new song, saying, Thou art worthy to take the book and to open the seals. He that sat was to look like a jasper and a sardine stone. But his fate casts no adverse reflection. It also testifies when squeezed or stepped on they explode. As Conor Cruise O'Brien has the heavens the stars the mountains. A measure of wheat for a penny. Crisp sales in recent weeks have shown a marked increase and the third part of the stars; so as the third part of them was darkened. Salt 'n' Vinegar flavour crisps. And the day shown an unkind critic. The name of the star is called Wormwood.

THREE NOTABLE FICTION REISSUES

The name of the Company has been changed. Those entrants who had the effrontery, reflecting the intention, were not so much part of this competition as to become major snack and related product manufacturers. As for the brave spirit who defined Day Vid Frost as an Israel crop failure, we suggest he patents it immediately. We are now placing a new emphasis on expansion. The Viet-Cong predictably served as an excuse. And we shall be watching out. Ram Shackle, the Indian beggar. Which will also fit in. Two olive trees. Two candle sticks. A thousand two hundred and threescore days. There have been three notable fiction reissues in recent weeks. The latest trade figures illustrate the short-run cost to the balance of payments, dearer oil, smaller exports and the delay in the shipment of goods. Others will go later. But now. A : 8)… Qa5 ? ? ; 9) ab : !, Qal : ; 10) ktb3, etc.

THE JEWISH QUESTION

COVENTRY COMMUNITY ROYAL BBC. This post is open to Village Halls and Playing Fields. Grade I of the Scales. Head Night Porter. Educated "A" levels or good "O". Want to be needed? Between the ages of 18 and Rd3, c6 ; 10) Rd8, e2 ; Each holiday home Ward Aides, PA/SEC. head Jewish question, essential qualification, internal. Experience committee.

BRITAIN CANNOT AFFORD WOMEN

Britain faces her worst winter sorrows of the shabby-genteel. The inescapable cost that nineteenth-century. It is surely unnecessary plaintively than in the novels of Simon Raven. The Government have few options, the boyhood of Fielding Gray, the freeze and squeeze, 'a bright nervous youth in his mid-twenties,' they have not yet begun to yield. In this fourth volume demand has still been restricted. Even this summer he was frustrated by a monstrous father. Sterling has not yet struggled entirely free of suspicion. Inns of Court or a Good Regiment as a desirable means. If the economy were stronger, Greek and Anglicanism, Christ and Socrates. Britain cannot afford women, they have different concepts of manliness. Ten thousand tinkers. Breda Claffey. The judge and his hangman.

TOPLESS FORESTRY AT GRIPS

Only the Forestry Commission, first female crush, breasts prominent but not outrageous, the conventional Irish types. But what the British Government must avoid, and this bare statement 'forced since childhood into a victim's pattern'. That Miss K can write as well as this makes the book's central failings all the more.

A BLOODBATH FOR LBJ

Concocting bootless 'anti-riot' programmes NCNP was white from the beginning, failing to recognize that diffuse anger was going to waste a great deal of money such as a fire hydrant being turned off on a hot day. Last autumn, in the general elections, NCNP candidates hardly made a dent at all. A 'bloodbath' was expected, and perhaps even do something about Lyndon Johnson. There was only an 'eruption'.

NAKED AT THE COUNCIL TABLE

Seen from Whitehall, of course, the survival of Israel was a marginal concern. This was the aspect that tickled the fancy of journalists and diplomatists. Secret treaties! An important go-between was briefed by a British Minister 'over lunch at the Savile Club'. Doing away with the bomb without conditions, he exclaimed, meant 'sending the British Foreign Secretary naked into the Council Chamber!' To the British, of course, other things mattered more at the time: principally the survival of the Empire. Nahas was a throwback to the age of Farouk, the fat playboy whom Whitehall had kept on the throne as a safeguard against nationalism. Who knows by 1977 the UN – under a different Secretary-General may actually be able to respond by bringing the pillars of the Temple down upon their heads.

I have many names. At the moment they are following Simon S. Fox Jr. The time is 14.4 hours, Central Standard Time. 73 degrees outside. Area 158,693 square miles, of which 1,890 square miles are water; ranks third. Golden eye of the automatic light rests between my fingers. Billboards and autopsies. Natural endowments are included in 20 million acres of public reservations. All outdoor sports are possible. Deep sea sleeping, and angling for small game are favourite pastimes. Eyes fall away to 282 feet below sea level. I am being hunted by bear, mountain lions, elk and deer. Duck, pheasant, rabbit, dove and quail. Meanwhile I eat a toasted cheese hamburger. My lips are frenchfries teasing cole slaw fingers. My belly is a Golden Poppy and the Motto is I have Found It. Or as posted to my three wives. Ranked according to value

Vehicles

food

allied products

fabricated metal

machinery

stone
clay
glass
lumber and apparel.

White gold her face one of my names married. A bevy
of stars, some now fallen. Originally a day's journey
apart. Reproductions. A gristmill, wine press and the
reservoir with its undershot waterwheel. Are stored
chapel and adjoining wing of seven rooms she lives in
now with the fourth husband of my second wife. Under
the roughhewn redwood roof timbers they are lashed
together with rawhide. Open during daylight hours
an unusual arrangement of garden pools. Hours subject to change in summer. No dogs, with the exception
of seeing-eye dogs, are allowed. Cats are permitted to
stay overnight provided they are on leash. A naturalist
is on duty. As members of the 89-person party died,
those remaining resorted to cannibalism. Only 47 were
rescued. Picnicking. Campsites near the original area.
Where I waited.
Cement
sand
gravel and stone
and a gun.

They knew I was there. They waited. It was a matter of
impatience between them and me, between the sunken
gardens, the colonnade and the workshop. They set up

their own quarantine regulations. Frozen chickens and yoghourt were delivered from the nearest supermarket. She played the mechanical organ, he an old horse fiddle, and other games with other interesting relics. Most of their amusements can be accommodated. With or without the presence of Simon S. Fox Jr. So I emerged from an underground channel through different rock strata. It was when hitting Highway 101 I noticed I was being followed. I turned off into a winding road. Without campsites

rest areas

picnicking

trailer hookups

Naturalist program.

Only their faces, glass faces behind me, twisted into grotesque shapes by the Pacific winds. Surrounded by Himalayan cedars, illuminated with 8,000 coloured lights. I proceeded with lights extinguished for almost a mile, and began a futuristic transit system to the moon. An atomic submarine, scientifically authentic, to view mermaids, sea serpents, the face of my first wife. And her father. Pets may be left in the kennel at the main gate, he said. But the cat is dead, I replied. In that case we will arrange a funeral at once. But I didn't want her buried just then, after all she was my first pet and liked me to do things with her poodle hair. However I told him that eventually a statue in her honour would be appropriate for erection in the town park, where visitors may choose to arrive by helicopters. He seemed genuinely pleased at this idea and showed me around the grounds. Crocodiles, hippopotami and snakes slipped through murky water. Along the shore, amid live, rare, tropical trees, shrubs and flowers, appeared elephants and other jungle animals. Visitors, he said, you know will find it hard to believe that none of the animals are alive. I knew he was renowned for his hospitality, wines and thoroughbred horses. I asked to be shown the champagne plant, wine cellars and bottling rooms. He showed me his study built in the shape of a wine barrel. And a photo of his daughter in graduation drag.

Other photos of his home town
pharmacy
ice cream parlor
bank
drugstore
dentist's office
general store
an old oil rig
early locomotive
box-car
handcar and caboose
hotel
saloon and other enterprises.

Lucinda, my first wife to be, chewed chewing gum in the memorial garden of camellias, roses and flowering shrubs. That's the orchard over there a fine sight to see you know, he said, the Cherry Picking Festival is held in June and the public is invited to pick their own fruit and over there well we have the Marine Corps Supply Depot – there we go you know my grandmother or was it my great grandfather was Celtic see that fireplace well it's modeled after a Scottish war lord's and this well it's a miniature Railway an authentic replica of an oldtime coal-burning engine and that well that's a photo of the world's largest jet-missile-rocket test centers and has a 22-mile runway – not open to visitors of course.

I saw her petrified face imprinted on fossilized leaves. Later at a health resort under the hot-water geysers we made it for the first time in the mineral springs and mineralized mud baths. My mouth searching for hers by means of siphon pipes. Later that night I got a strange blow-job in a parking-lot, it was 35 degrees outside, by a weird woman. Two days later I was still weak at the knees and couldn't think about it. Now I could try and ease my way out of this by saying I didn't ask questions, just stated my attitudes

Read for pleasure

Consider myself informed

Education is important

Enjoy making decisions

Sense of humor is important

Enjoy discussing ideas

My best work is done alone

I am ambitious

Have travelled extensively

Spent most of my life in a city

Prefer to live in a large city
I make friends easily
I am dominant
Relationship with my family is fucked up
I am sophisticated
Considered attractive
Interested in marriage
Liberal regarding sex
I am politically interested
I often rebel at authority
I am more of a dove than a hawk
War is morally wrong
My date should be psychologically stronger
I am optimistic
Pot and pop-pills are morally right
I drink regularly

Fantasy Profile

Organized	Dreamer	Athletic	Sexy
Confident	Aggressive	Subtle	Natural
Practical	Well dressed	Healthy	Introverted
Passionate	Thrifty	Quiet	Nervous
Funny	Warm	Paternal	Extroverted
Serious	Impulsive	Talkative	Trusting
Active	Intelligent	Kind	Content
Maternal	Cheerful	Creative	Self-controlled
Cautious	Do-It-Yourself	Altruistic	Emotional
Reflective	Jealous	Flirtatious	Wholesome

Common Interests

Pets	Shopping	Long car trips
Parties	Creative writing	Local politics
Lectures	Walking	Photography
Medicine	Jazz	Psychology
Stereo equipment	Scientific journals	E.S.P.
Acting	Movies	Stock Market
Modern literature	Yoga	Antiques
Discotheques	Humanities	Astrology
Ethics	Dancing	Pool
Pop Art	Outdoor sports	Camping

My special interests
   Living out other peoples' fantasies.

Still what have I managed to say? That this is a performance of extraordinary charm and brilliant technique. And though there are dozens of qualities I value more, this production embodies its own vision as completely as any I have ever seen. Certainly Lucinda had some of these qualities, qualifications and I recognise now that serious, impulsive, talkative, trusting face following me round every bend. Along the northeastern edge of the city. Round the remains of the 11 feet in diameter valley oak, killed by miners digging around its roots for gold. Of course she failed to recognise me then as they both marvelled at the two pieces of tree preserved in the monument. But as soon as I got in the chevy they began the chase again.

A broad expanse of white sand beach, bordered by Monterey cypress trees. I had left the chevy in a prominent place outside the motel. When I went back I noticed they had changed their name in the register. I recognised his cramped handwriting. Through the keyhole I watched them doing Yoga together. Why had she never done that with me? Admittedly there had been some extraordinary positions we discovered on fossil beds. Extensive asbestos underlying the area. Through another keyhole I had watched my second beloved wife being whipped with kippers. Why had she never told me? I knew she liked me licking liquor out of her. The kippers were never, of course, mentioned in the divorce proceedings, her Attorney was an understanding guy, or so she informed me in the middle of one of our last fights. She also informed me that he liked fishing for
black bass
bluegill
crappie
and catfish
He came from a once booming mining town, complete with plaza and hanging tree. His father kept a saloon sporting batwing doors, housing firearms, coins, minerals and other documents, papers of historical interest. I always knew she had an interest in antiques. He was

well-preserved. I guess, for his age. Maybe the dieting the Yoga helped. Certainly they managed to keep me awake half the night, why hadn't she ever moaned like that with me?

I mapped out the next day's route, making sure to supply myself with extra water. The thought of the three of us splitting into frantic parties, each striving wildly to get out of the barren valley finally made me have a peaceful sleep for four hours.

The weather Bureau reported it had been as high as 120 degrees for days in succession. At sunrise I turned off the main road and started crossing the valley. I could see they were hesitant, he hunched over the wheel, while she sat on a bench in the picnicking area, scraping off her already dry pancake makeup. Soon I couldn't see them at all for the rising dust. Then dream shapes formed out of the desert, their buick floated a few miles behind me. I didn't have the energy or patience to view the wealth of geological phenomena, but was well aware of every one of the geological divisions of time, of the space that widened, narrowed between them and myself. Memories held together by the thinnest of threads, nevertheless self-contained and delicious

sunny

boisterous

ironic

they melted, melded and interfused with swoops of greens, reds, oranges. Instead of a battle-field, the arena

became a dance floor, which did not in any way allevi-
ate or moderate the risks involved. Memories that used
to communicate a violent anxiety in the valley created
an airy sense of freedom, light and light-heartedness.
Texture, trigger, all tonality pink, soft and glowing. At
one point outside a ghost town I thought yes I could die
here quite happily, no longer confuse the mainspring of
the movement with the movement. And Lucinda would
lie on top of me a tortured Earth Goddess with her
magazine advertisement mouth closed forever. Smooth,
resolved and beautiful. This simple remedy carried me
through an hour or so. Now I enjoy violence as much
as the next guy, but enough is enough. Five days is
plenty for the most exciting series, and with the heat
penetrating my brain wires, itching my balls, I decided to
turn back. I passed them at 100 m.p.h. Not even having
time to see their white sun sunken faces turn crimson.
This is the sin of sins against an awkward power structure, I thought, the refusal really to take it seriously.
However I still had the gun, though unloaded, in case
of any unforeseen advantage on their side. They after
all seemed to take the whole thing very seriously. That
worried me. The fact that I could foresee them as a lost
patrol chasing their chartered souls through endless
deserts. But I would wave a flag, arrange for a brass band
to play When Johnnie Comes Marching Home, bring
extra noisemakers and confetti, drink beer, kiss girls.
There'd be songs, dancing, music, flowers, hundreds of
celebrities, like

Ho Chi Minh

Betty Grable

Lyndon Johnson

Regis Toomey

and John Wayne rising out of their ghost towns. A spiritual balance regained. Weren't those the words she used once as we lay sunning ourselves on her daddy's swimmingpool terrace? I didn't believe in her soul-saving outfit, at least not until she undid her leather bikini No I don't want to save your soul Simon I want to save your ass. She was on one of her amphetamine trips then, and possibly taking some now five miles behind, before sucking him off to keep his driving spirits up.

VISITORS SHOULD DRINK FROM CLEARLY MARKED SPRINGS.

I got out of the car and stood at the mouth of a creek. At the visitor center I noticed that daytime hourly slide shows were featured

Mountains

Canyons

Former centers of mining activities

Crystal-like salt formations

Salt pools with crystals forming on their surfaces

Sand dunes

Beehive charcoal kilns

Deteriorated mining towns

I slid through the air-conditioned dark into the blinding yellow. They must have passed by, possibly back on the main road, having an argument. I thought I could even then hear Lucinda's hysterical voice, but it was a horse neighing. Her voice, her mother's above the wedding march, The bride wore a traditional long-sleeved full-length white satin wedding dress and her seven bridesmaids were in white silk dresses trimmed with goya red velvet ribbons (subdued lest they clashed with the bridegroom's resplendent full dress uniform). The makeup man had shaved the bride's eyebrows, waxed her hairline to change the shape of her face. Raised and arched her eyebrows to open her eyes and used two and a half sets of eyelashes. Shaded her nose to make it look smaller and soften the lines around her mouth and shaded her cheeks. There was a six foot wedding cake and 5,000 dollars' worth of champagne had been ordered. So the newspapers accounted for their wedding. The mother's face a wreath of smiles, At last my daughter has decided to keep the good life rolling in high gear. Our elopement had never been even condescended to. Without emerging from our seven dollars a day cave on the ninth floor of a hotel we bribed them by call and collect. At least Lucinda did, Oh leave it to me honey daddy will come round. Fugitive lovers. She enjoyed it more. The phone calls, cables, letters. Demands. Commands. Finally after a week the chauffeured limousine arrived with a note All Is Forgiven Come Home. She went. I remained until another week went by and the limousine arrived with Lucinda between her parents, looking at though she'd come to pick up a corpse. I'm pregnant. She said, as I climbed in next to their negro chauffeur.

We were married at the nearest registry place that also catered for cremations. No five-tiered pound cake then topped by sugar-spun basket. No calligraphers, their labors done, studied their handiwork on 500 invitations and 'carriage cards' (for parking assignments). No aides clocked the ceremony in advance. Her father handed me the ring. Over in a few minutes. The divorce, a year later, took a little longer. About a day. I wasn't present. Her father's letter ended with the words No man need be our enemy, no one's interests need be forgotten. Because ours is the strength, ours also must be the generosity. I didn't cash the check but used it for other purposes and returned it to him. I pictured him appearing in the windowless second floor briefing room. Independence of expression has now become almost unthinkable. Determine what forces are required and procure and support them as economically as possible. The whole episode with Lucinda was fragmented into a honeycomb of separate actions. The mock histrionics where her father prostrated himself before me, dug his nose in the rug and moaned Look Si please do what I say give up Lucy and you'll have an income of

Plot can diminish in a forest of effects and accidents. Motivations can be done away with, loose ends ignored, as the son-in-law, in effect, is invited to become the father-in-law's collaborator, filling in the gaps he left out.

   We lived in the annex, or tried to live. I took up
writing
painting
sculpture
photography
athletics
Zen
Judo
Karate
movie making
stocks and shares
while Lucinda knitted pink and blue baby outfits, and
watched television. All night movies. Sleeping, com-
plained of feeling sick, headachey during the day. I'd
go for long car trips, check in at some obscure motel,
get drunk for several days, until the limousine caught
up with me, the chauffeur lifting me into the car, up to
the briefing room, where the old man paced the walled
room, lighting relighting huge cigars, offering me one,
knowing I'd refuse. Refuse the terms, conditions, decisions. Look Si I think it's about time you

The sweat ran down my spine, chest, between my legs.
The extra water had run out. I started seeing
unmarked springs
avocado groves
fertile islands
a honeycomb of waterways
mammoth lakes

sheer walls of symmetrical blue-grey basaltic columns
crystal-clear hot springs
six packs of fridged beer
641,000 acres of lakestrewn land
sea life housing 13 large glass tanks
a 90-foot pool with perforated seals
Aquarium with prostrate mermaids
20 to 30 feet high snowdrifts
65 underground rooms
gardens
grottos
swimmingpools
white marble statuary
stained-glass windows under water
white, conical 115-foot towers
sanctuary of aquatic birds

I passed some tourists dune-buggying in their Bermuda gear. I noticed I was running out of gas. Perhaps they had also, maybe they hadn't reached the main highway after all. I would pass them, wave cheerfully at Lucinda stretched out in semi-consciousness in the back seat, while he would be trudging through the desert. Want some help? I'd call out as my chevy churned up dust in his sweaty puffy red face. Later I'd visit her shrine. And all the rest the Wee Kirk o' the Heather reproduction of the church where Annie Laurie worshipped.

Reproduction of the church where Gray wrote his Elegy Written in a Country Churchyard. And attend the

hourly lecture on The Last Supper. The Hall of Cruci-
fixion, measuring 45 by 195 feet. Note that visitors must
remain during the showing, and passing out as the
lecturer got to the 180th part of Christ's body.

The gas gauge hovered over the E where my eyes
constantly attached themselves. My mouth seemed made
of sand. My whole body a sinking dune buggying itself
back, forward from the steering wheel. Then I saw their
car off to the right. They were nowhere to be seen. Hiding
perhaps in the back, the gun loaded, waiting, ready to
leap out. The bloody ending as inevitable as the climax of
a Greek tragedy. Or so Lucinda would want. The episode
could hardly be bettered: the vaporous, honey-coloured
scene as my body would writhe to earth in a quarter-time
choreography of death. The tone of the scene shifting
in a split second from humor to horror as the blood-
ied victim attempted to aim his gun, forgetting it was
unloaded. And after the affair had been discreetly seen
to, they would trade in the buick one afternoon for the
same model in another color, borrowing her father's
chauffeur to trundle it through the desert until it had
accumulated the early mileage. She might come out in
hives, her usual accessory to any crisis, and her mother
applies glycerine furiously over her daughter's body,
collaborating that Men are Terrible just Beasts. And for
several nights she'd be frigid in their king-sized bed.

Ah that bed, and others larger, smaller, narrow, wide
around which we played our games. I the dwarf, she

the Queen. She my sister. I was the President. She a
slave
prostitute
movie star
nymphet
lesbian
And myself a Pimp
Judge
Flagellist
We arrived at a point when even words were unnecessary. A record collection when each piece of music ful-
filled the appropriate background. Head full of musical
organs. Feet scaled the walls, the strips of light placed
between the toes. Her ears were sitars blown by my
carved mouth. Sitting in the shower spinning fantasies
on to her face, plucking at myself, the feathers of geese
and quail from thigh to neck. Upsidedown. From right
to left. Turning her over in the flat of my dreams. Her
mother waved from a desert tower. Her father lay on a
bundle of stocks and shares directing the family traffic
through glass stairways. I stripped a banana thrust it up
her cunt, half way, ate the rest, poured sour cream over
her and buried my fingers in the remaining pink areas.
Her feet followed the trail of foxes in snow. Markings of
spiders along ridges memories slipped into.

More than 100 life-sized figures in 35 scenes. Hand
and footprints imprinted in a coral-like crust deposited
by the waters of an ancient sea. In my sophomore year I

was considered a clean-cut boy, permitted by girls to go so far if I was on a leash, crated or otherwise physically restricted at all times. A thirty minute color slide show on the cultivation and history of dates. A riot of color. A series of leap-frog bridges. Blind closets, trapdoors and secret passageways. A huge overshot redwood wheel. An acre of grotesquely knotted thoughts, accessible only by foot or horseback; no roads had been cut into the wilderness not then in my sophomore year.

Thoughts now encounter shelves of ideals from these enormous arcs of nostalgia 50 feet in the arc. A large depression whose floor is scarred by numerous projections. It was about that time I guess, due to subnormal daily activities the content of dreams became so dense that the only life within them consisted of small briny shrimp and the pupae of the ephydrid fly, I began then to organise a free-form dimensional equipment in the shape of a bucket. Digging below the surface the continuous bucket line operated 24 hours a day, except on July 4th and December 25th, and I viewed the dredge, as I continue to do so, from a foreign land.

NEVER TRUST A MAN WHO
BATHES WITH HIS FINGERNAILS

He was a small man. Half Cherokee. His
movements, silences were those of the Indian.
The women watched, roused, a little
frightened. The husband of one of the women,
lover of the other, also watched. From a
distance, watched from his studio as the man
hammered into wood, did odd jobs around the
house. Outside, looking in at the women.
The wife's movements became lighter. She
laughed more. Her face flushed from the ride
on his motorbike, through light rain off the
mountains. She crouched behind his warmth.
This warmth in her cheeks, eyes, spread as
they sat in front of the fire, quietly talking,
or letting the wood speak. The other woman
waited, wanting to make a third of this situation also. Not sure of her sense of place,
the placing of where she might sit, walk,
sleep between husband and wife. Wife. Husband.

And when the husband entered the room he
hesitated. 'I think we might have a door here,'
he said, gesturing at the space between kitchen
and bedroom, 'what do you think – could you do
that?' The man nodded, hands lightly rested
on his knees. The wife bent over sewing,
hair, still wet, hid her face. The other looked
at the husband, the other two. Out of the
window, at the aspens, the cloud shadows
gathering speed through the valley. Back again
to the interior of light and shade, where
the three sat, moved from room to room.
Rooms without doors. Except the studio the
husband climbed into, shut down the door,
stared at blank paper in the typewriter,
listened to the wood sawing, the man's low
whistling. And the wife's laughter.

He arrived on his motorbike, a low black
figure, part of the machine. He seemed larger
then, the wife thought, as she looked out
of the kitchen window, each morning at eight
o'clock. Her hands paused over the sink.
Off the machine, he waved. His hand recon-
structing the speed, weather, landscape he
had passed through. The husband bent over
his typewriter, pulled out a page, crushed it,
and threw into the wastepaper basket. 'Damn
it he's just a bum – been here a week now and

what has he done – what are we paying him
for?' 'But he's nearly finished the
windows – I know he's slow but he knows what
he's doing – besides we are paying him only
what a soda jerk would earn,' the wife
answered, quietly smiling, quietly going on
with bread making, her fingers feeling, weighing
the elasticity of the dough. 'It's all very
well but I think we ought to have a time
sheet for him – always this impression he
gives of unlimited time – the last job he
had he was fired – there he was when this couple
drove up – apparently he swung the axe into
the wood when he saw them – the only work
he'd done all day – no – I'll get a time sheet.'
So the husband drew up a time sheet, which
he nailed on the adobe wall, which the man
marked with small black crosses.

   He ate with them, sitting between the
women. The husband at the head of the table.
The women talked. The men ate. 'How about
all of us going to that hot spring pool tomorrow –
you can show us where it is – you've been there?'
The wife said. The man nodded, pushed his
bread around the plate, 'it is small – but
the water is great – good for the body,' he said.
But it's a long walk isn't it – we can't take
the car all the way down there?' the husband

paused in eating, looked at the women.
'Oh we don't mind walking – it will be lovely
you'll see – oh it will be so good,' the wife went
on eating quickly, giggling slightly, 'and we'll
do it in the nude.' The other woman felt her
own weight sink into the chair, felt the weight
of the husband's eyes, his face whiter then in
the afternoon light. The man next to her was
motionless, hands again on his knees, dark
skin shining, grains of dirt almost a lighter
shade.

The women cleared the table. The husband
climbed into his work. The man measured the
space for the door. While the women washed,
dried the dishes, their heads bent low, close
together. The wife quick, with a quicker
laughter than the other, who laughed slowly in
the spaces of the wife's laughter. The silence
coming from the room above them, she later
entered, when the wife went shopping. A
quickness then between them on his studio
couch, listening for the car rattling over
the bridge, and all the while below them the
lower sound of nails slowly driven into wood,
the man's whistling louder. The louder noises
of the wife returning, putting things in
cupboards, banging of dishes, as they straightened
their clothes, the couch cover. He lifted up

the door for her to clutch her way down into
the kitchen, into the bathroom where she powdered
over the heightened colour of her face.

    The man went on hammering, hummed, bent
into his work. The typewriter a jerky rhythm
above. The wife talked, her voice higher
pitched, movements quicker from cupboard to
table, from table to cupboard. 'Can I help?'
the other asked, standing behind the table,
her hands becoming steady from the firmness of
wood, the stone wall behind her. 'I'll show
you how to make stuffed pimentos and cabbage,'
the wife said. 'Oh yes that would be nice.'
She came round to where the wife bent over the
vegetables, watched the deftness of knife against
green, red, slicing into, through, pulling out
the seeds. The hammering a steady sound. The
typewriter paused, went on, paused, while the
women worked with sharp knives.

    He did not arrive at eight the next morning.
Thunder stirred over the distant mountains.
A sirocco wind spiralled sand in the desert.
Three spirals on their own, that approached,
joined up into a whirling tower of sand. Stilts
of rain came slowly down the mountains, faster
over the valley. Apples were flung on to the
ground, some breaking open on the cracked dry

earth under the wet surface. 'He's holding
off until the storm passes I guess – oh I hope
it clears up did so want to make that hot spring
today,' the wife said, 'he did say today didn't
he – he didn't say he wouldn't be working today?'
'Lazy bastard,' the husband muttered, then in a
louder tone, 'it won't clear up look at those
clouds piling up there on those mountains.'
He went up into the studio, and put the radio
on very loudly. So loud that none of them heard
the motorbike crossing the bridge. Though the
wife looking out at the sky changing, small
patches of blue that widened, edged off the
clouds either side of the mountains, mesas,
saw the large black shape hurled,
suddenly from that clear space between clouds,
river and the trees. 'There – here he is,' she
shouted. 'What?' shouted the husband from
the opening at the top of the stairs. 'He's
here – get ready – it's clearing we can go after
all,' she shouted back while opening the front
door. The man approached, his heavy boots
hardly made any sound. He stood in the porch-
way, shaking off the rain, rain over his goggles,
eyes, hair. She began rubbing his head with a
towel, but he took it gently from her. 'Oh
you are soaked through – you better change
you can wear something of his – though nothing
I guess will fit.' He stood between the women,

when the husband swung down the stairs. He rubbed himself quickly then, and put back his shirt. 'But that's wet,' the wife said. He shrugged, 'It doesn't matter I feel warm enough.' 'Well are we going or not?' the husband asked, not looking at the three, seeming to look with concentration at the half finished dishes stacked. 'Of course we're going – look it's going to be a beautiful day.' 'Very well don't blame me if we get caught in a storm.'

The men sat in front. The women at the back. The husband drove, and manoeuvred the rear mirror until he could see his wife's face. His own, he knew, had a strange pallor, and his hands, gripping the steering wheel, paler, next to the other, whose darkness was darker, glistening there on his knees. They drove in silence along the valley road, turned off, and bumped across the desert. 'You'll soon have to stop,' the man said. Where – here – there – where?' the husband asked. 'See those rocks over there well there – it's a few miles down to the river – there's a small track we can take.' The husband brought the car to an abrupt halt. They all climbed out. 'Did you bring any towels for drying ourselves?' the husband asked his wife. 'Oh the sun will dry us,' she replied, walking quickly on, following the man. 'I brought

one,' the other woman said, as she caught up
with the husband. She glanced at him, but he
looked ahead, to where the other two now were
at some distance, then they disappeared round
the larger rocks. He quickened his pace. She
tried to keep up, and stumbled. He caught hold
of her hand, released. She fell back, breathing
heavily. 'Where have they gone I can't see
them?' His face red now, as they clambered
on over large stones, dry grass, sand. She
looked back at the mountain range, clear cut
against the expanse of blue, the car, a fallen
grey object, in the desert.

They turned the corner and saw the river,
a thin strip of steel from that distance.
'They must have run down here,' he said, and
slowed up, waited for her to be beside him.
She stooped and looked down over the yellow
boulders, then up at his face, further up
into the sky that narrowed as they went on
down the track.

She saw his clothes on a flat piece of
rock, but could not see the man anywhere.
The wife's face appeared over some bushes.
'Isn't it lovely here – so warm – so quiet.'
She stepped out, naked, her arms raised,
hair tossed back, as she climbed over the

rocks and disappeared. The husband slowly
undressed. The woman did likewise. She
followed him over the rocks, slipping a little,
feeling the sun between heavy breasts,
she clutched the towel. 'Here we are – it's
terribly small – but I think there's room for
us all,' the wife shouted up from the narrow
pool, only her legs submerged in the water.
The man, his back towards her, thrust his face
under the jet of water that spurted out from
a small hole in the rocks. The husband stood
on the edge of the pool, 'Is there room do
you think?' he asked. The other woman quickly
got in between the man, the wife. She tried
getting the whole of her body submerged.
The man shifted slightly, his mouth open. The
husband lay half on the edge, half on his wife's
body. They lay there, shifted around, attempted
to move, manoeuvre their bodies, without
touching. The women looked down at the men from
the corners of their eyes, while the water
bubbled below, and behind them. The river, dark
green in parts, moved slowly.

    The man got out first, went over and sat on
a large rock, facing the river. The husband
now lay between the women, his head
back under the hot water. The women climbed
out, and went to another rock, the other side

from where the man sat. The wife, laughing
quietly, stretched out, and through half closed
eyes watched the man, watched her husband. The
other woman wrapped the towel around herself,
and watched the patterns of light on her legs,
rocks, on the wife's back.

The husband joined them, sat between them.
He smiled, smiled at his largeness, at the smaller,
almost childish, hairless body of the other man,
the other side of the pool, who started scratching
the grime off his body, digging this out from his
nails, picking out the dirt slowly, carefully.
'He certainly makes use of the people he works
for – and just look now what's he's doing – never
trust a man who…' the husband whispered, lay
back, his head resting on his wife's legs, then
against the other's breasts. The women laughed.
'You just never stop – do you,' the wife said,
'at least he doesn't say things the way you do.'
'Ha you think his silences are profound or
something – he's dumb – hasn't a thought in
his head – he just drifts – think of that woman
of his respecting his silence when he came back
and found her living with another man – what did
he do – go away and wait – no – I mean there's
all sorts of places to wait but to wait in the
backyard I mean to say what kind of man is that.'
He closed his eyes, sighed. They all closed

their eyes, allowed their hands to wander, rest
in places, parts, spread out on the flat rock.

The wife sat up suddenly, 'where's he gone
he's disappeared?' The husband, his eyes
remained closed, laughed, 'Ah he's got the message
at last.' The other woman opened the towel a
little, and allowed her weight to be part of the
rock's weight. The wife stood up, looked over
and beyond where the man had been. 'Do you think
he feels outside it all?' Oh he's all right –
he's the sort that likes to go off on his own
he'll be back soon enough,' the husband said,
pulling his wife down on top of him. 'Not here
not now – might come back,' she said, giggling,
thrusting him away. He mouthed the other's
body, neck, his hands feeling the softer skin,
the flushed parts from the water.

They did not hear the man returning. He
squatted the other side of the pool, his head
bent, hands hung limply between his legs. The
wife saw him first, saw his small curved brown
back, glistening. He looked round then, and
grinned, small neat white teeth flashed up at
her from across the pool. She looked at the
other two, the woman who had discarded
the towel, her breasts, thighs already a harsh
red against the whiteness. Her husband's head

rested against the woman. 'I'm going into
the pool again,' the wife said, and scrambled
down, arched her body under the jet of hot
water. The man humming softly, began cleaning
his toe nails.

The husband jerked up, looked down into
the pool, across the pool. 'He should keep his
dirty habits to himself,' he whispered. The
woman, smiled, brought the towel across herself,
it was just wide enough to cover the parts touched
by the sun. The wife lay half asleep in the
water. The man went on picking out bits of dirt
from his nails. The husband shifted around on
the rock, so that his back faced the pool, his
wife, the man and the other woman.

The river became a darker green by the time
they dressed. They climbed back slowly, up the
track, in single file. The man first, the wife
followed, followed by the husband, the woman
last. They walked in silence, only the sound
of the river gurgling, and then the wind bringing
dust and sand as they turned the corner, and moved
out of the canyon.

'Well I didn't think much of this hot spring
pool – I mean I thought at least it would be
larger,' the husband said, as he started the car

up, as they waited for the man, who had fallen
out of line, to step behind a bush. The wife
did not say anything. 'It wasn't so bad but maybe
next time just the three of us will come,' the
other woman said. They gazed out of the window,
and watched the man move slowly towards them.

EYES THAT WATCH
BEHIND THE WIND

What was happening?
She no longer knew. Feeling only her pain. And his.
The weight.

Pulse in the stone
wanting to hear it. See it. Not enclosed. But see and hear
it emerge from the skin. Transparent. For the touch. Like
the necklace of delicate pink shells round her, hanging
over one breast. But even these she knew would break
soon enough. She liked holding them, one by one. The
smell of sea. This naked back caught by light. Ocean
reflected. Mountains of waves rolled them together,
separated them on to the beach. Breaking out of the
sand he had been buried under. Her own burial with
the branches, twigs he had put in, without her knowing.
When opening her eyes she saw arrows pierced into her
body under the sand mount.

The memory of this
and the wreath of white flowers high on some rocks
facing the ocean, she had suddenly seen one morning,
after sheltering in a cave. A cave she had left quickly

because of two fishermen who leered at her from some rocks nearby.

They had been in Mexico nearly three months. Moved into, out of three places. Yet she had no sense of placement with him. For him. There had been once, but that was hard to recall. And if remembered only fell heavily between them.

A longing
for rain. Heavy rain through the night. They were told it was the rainy season. The days continued hot, dusty, oppressive. Mountains seemed to be pushing their way nearer. Or being pushed by thick white clouds clinging there. The only clouds.

On their way to Cuetzalan, south of Mexico City, they had passed the cone shaped volcano Popocatepetl contemplating Ixtaccihuatl, the White Woman. Snow covered belly and thighs. The outlines of these volcanoes were not visible. Sometimes even their heads disappeared, then reappeared, risen islands floating high above them, where stars must have been, and clouds formed smoke columns above the snow.

Ixtaccihuatl

Popocatepetl watching
watching behind the wind eruptions under skin. Under eyes. Of those who wore slick neat city suits, who stepped heavily along the hot concrete. She was glad to leave that. Glad not to be furtively looked at by those dark shells.

Eyes never meeting her own.

Glad she would perhaps no longer hear the word 'Gringos' shouted out. Or be spat at by passing drunks. Clutched by beggars. Stoned by boys. Be confronted by huddled shanties in front of middle-class apartment boxes. Confronted by her own strangeness, helplessness in the face of their defeat, their resigned acceptance of life conquered by death. The family of God knows how many living in cramped quarters, who smiled cheerfully at her. The girl of nineteen who had just given birth to her third child. She found it hard to smile, feeling self-conscious of her clothes, the difference in their lives. The simplicity yet hardness of theirs. The complexity and softness of her own.

They arrived in Cuetzalan, a town appearing to be from another century. High up in the mountains, where walking through clouds seemed more than a possibility. A place once invaded by the French, driven out by the Totanaca Indians. She liked it, admired at once their dignity, openness. Their immaculate white clothes. Women in long skirts, brightly embroidered sashes, lace blouses, purple, green yarns of wool twisted into their dark hair, piled high on top of their heads. Some carried babies on their backs, in baskets of string woven on to wood, supported by a strap around their foreheads. Yes, she felt self-conscious, conspicuous in her short dress, and they were curious, but they nodded, smiled, spoke gently: *Adiós Adiós. Buenos días. Buenas noches.* The soft padding of the men's sandalled feet. The firm tread of the women's naked feet.

Part of the earth.

They at least had accepted, made use of the land. Had no use for, no need to fill in the Void like the Mexicans did with noise. The sound of radios. Music relayed from a gramophone through a loudspeaker in the belfry tower, that started at 6 a.m. every day, and continued most afternoons. The town had, in fact, only had electricity for a year. The Mexicans loved their new toy. A television set was a proud possession.

Once, going for a walk along one of the many stony tracks, passed by white clad Indians bent double with their load of sugar cane, following their mules also laden with cane, or long heavy planks of wood, she heard from a wooden shack the sounds of Louis Armstrong. Again a loss of placement. The sound reminding her, taking her back. Forward. The knowledge that soon she would cross the border to a country, his country America, where once more she would feel a stranger.

And England?

How distant it seemed now. Yet in moments a longing.

But for what?

She had no sense of belonging there either. A vague feeling of 'roots'. A certain kind of identity. The freedom of knowing her way around. But the greyness. Oh that grey, grey thing creeping from the sky, smoke, buildings, into the pores of skin. Grey faces. No she could not go back to that.

And here

well here there was a stillness, a gradual regaining from the landscape. The maize as tall as trees. Bananas unripe, and oranges. Coffee plantations surrounded by mountains, layers of deep blue fading into clouds, mist. Shrillness of insects. Locusts. A startling brightness from the poinsettia, flowers of Christmas Eve, above her head bent low. Now high, watching the turkey buzzards circle, in their search for snakes. Then down at the line of leaf-cutter ants coming and going. Armies of them. A moving line of leaves, twigs along the track, up over the rocks into a small dark hole.

Up the mountain into a cave.

The sense of this land, a kind of timelessness caught her often by the throat. The line at the top of her shoulder blades crossing the spine. The tension there.

Expectation of his touch.

The placing of his tongue, razor sharp. Could enter. Squaring her for that, feet together, head neither too high nor too low. To make the last pass of any series of passes in silence. To perform some act that would provide an emotional yet rational climax.

She tried fighting off the longings, demands for what had been. Tried moving with the Mexican sense of no midday. No evening.

En la mañana, en la tarde, en la noche.

Even in this 'out of the century' town she felt weighed down by some slow stirring thing. The very earth. Smell of hard dry cracked earth. Sweat. Urine. Heavy scent of flowers mixed with smoke from the factory where sugar cane was melted down. Smell of dry blood. Pigs slaughtered. Shrieking of a pig escaping, caught, pulled by a rope, tethered to a rock, still shrieking. How could people live with this, under it, under the midday heat beginning so early in the morning, without it all thrusting through, quickening the pulse like the hump of muscle rising from the neck of a fighting bull, which erects when the bull is angry. How could it not all make the hands quick to grasp the *machete* from the leather sheaf hanging always close, so close to a man's body. And strike. Slice through another's skin?

Mass in the morning. Massacre in the afternoon. The ritual. The exorcism. Hadn't she been all too aware of this at the first bull fight? The heavy wary, sometimes dazed bulls. The swift agility of the matadors. One or more unarmed with a cape, but carrying the banderillas, provoking a series of charges; running in zig-zags, or seeing how close they could approach the bull while playing, without provoking a charge. The banderillas discreetly decorated with coloured streamers, that looked like flowers. More and more of these soon sticking out of the bull. From under these streams of blood, mixed with sweat. Continual prancing, or rigidness yet fluid dance, of the matador in his skin-tight pants, heavily brocaded cape. Light-hearted airs, graces, smiling forcedly. Flowery style, lengthy repertoire, until finally she found herself also taken in by it all. Admiring the redondo of man and bull executing a complete circle. The decorative pass with the cape in which it was held by one extremity, swung so that it described a circle around the man. She almost forgot her earlier nausea at the matador's arrogance, his Hollywood smile. While the bull paused, blinded by dust, sun, blood. And panic. The *olés* of the crowd, or their hissing when a picador missed the bull when charging, and the point of the pic slipped over the bull's hide without tearing it.

The waiting of a picador, waiting for the bull to get close enough so he could place the pic properly, but the bull struck the solid wall of the mattress covering chest, right flank and belly of the picador's blindfolded horse. The horns going under, again and again, until man and horse toppled over with a thud. She had looked away then, choking back the vomit, not wanting the others, the Americans, she sat with, to know that she was 'chickening' out. When she looked up again to the dragging out of the horse by a trio of mules, she noticed several people's faces quite pale. She glanced at him, crouched forward. Yes, he could accept this. The death ritual.

The meeting place of challenge.

It was absolute. It was in silence. Especially the final act, as the matador furled the muleta, sighting along the sword, so that it formed a continuous line with his face and arm preparatory to the killing. The two facing each other. It was physical. Sensual almost. Yes, she could understand his fascination with a sensual kind of violence. Seeing it there in his face, watching intently every move man and bull made.

The pulse in his neck moved
a small creature, ready to jump out, seize her own neck that arched back, down, where she felt the ache. The ache at times of wanting this violence in him to break out. Devour her. Hurt me hurt me hurt me. But not in this way. Not in the heavy silence of them both facing each other, weapons concealed. The final turning away, not even in anger, but resentment.

The challenge not met.
At such time she almost wanted the frenzied shouts of an audience: *Anda* – Go on

Anda

Anda

Anda

Not this rejection.
She couldn't take it. Nor the verbal attacks. When words became only accusations slung at each other. If no words, then it was a sword-thrust that goes in on the bias so that the point of the sword comes out through the skin of the bull's flank.

The man did not go in straight at the moment of killing. She remembered vividly the six out of eight bulls suffering this prolonged death. Haemorrhage from the mouth. Not just one sword, but several having been badly placed, and entered the lungs. Neither did she want the sense of triumph. The *vuelta al ruedo*. The tour of the ring made by the matador who had killed perfectly.

But anything

anything rather than the silent anger hanging heavily like the afternoon heat, when even the sheets were a weight on her limbs. And the angles of his body jutted out – thick branches thrusting her to the edge of the bed. Her own arms crossed over, around her neck. Breasts.

The weight

a stone tied to an inside cord in her belly, turned, turned and twisted. The thud thud thudding of her heart. Reminding her of the Indians in New Mexico. Their drum beats. The pulse quickening, or slowing down accordingly.

Asking

Praying

Asking

The asking

the praying for rain. Touch of the hands. A lightness. Fingers in her hair. Fireflies coming in through the open shutters. Then the longer hold of his tongue in her. Her mouth of him. Tongue resting there. A way of knowing him. He had been unsure then. Not sure what she wanted. Needed. Thinking perhaps she had dozed off. Or had passed into one of her trances. Towards those trances he felt a kind of envy, a fear. Could not share. The body removed. That she had gone far out. Into some area he could not be placed in, or find a place there with her. But he had his own areas. His own crablike places. Once they had watched whole colonies of crabs down over the rocks. Cancer. His sign. He was fascinated. She was curious. What parallels could she perhaps discover? They seemed to move slowly, but in fact moved quickly. In order to move forward they had to move backwards.

It was precisely this movement that often startled her. The way he had of carrying the weight of the past. In himself. To himself. In moments she accepted. But resented the way he tossed his head, stomped off, without a word, into his studio. She had the feeling he dived in there as he had into the huge waves. Waves she was for the first time in her life frightened of. So she would remain, alone, on the beach, under the shaded thatched covering, waiting. Watching. And he'd emerge, flushed, triumphant. Not like now when that transparent quality of skin from water had somehow given way to a paleness, as if pressed down under many stones. Or covered by sand. But his eyes, mouth had been left uncovered in the burial. And when he had heaped the sand over her, patted it down around her neck, he left her head, face uncovered. The trance then had been quick in coming. She had nearly reached some point in space. A space in herself, yet outside her body, when she felt his mouth, warm, salty from sweat, sea, on her eyes. She was jerked out of an area into a place she did not recognize, and then she saw the arrows. Breaking out from these she ran.

Screaming silently
in a space she had so nearly found, but then filled in by the arrow points. She threw her body, no longer her own body it seemed, but just a body hurled out of the ground, into the mountains of water, she bent her head

under, rose up, bent again, and struggled out. Further out to higher and higher mountains. Away from the beach, where she knew he waited, watching, not quite knowing. Unsure again.

And if she returned?

If she chose not to, but moved on out into the ocean until perhaps the area she had so nearly reached could be touched upon.

Later when they touched, it was as if someone else touched her. She gave herself up to this. From out of the past, with lovers she would not see again, be committed to. It was new. The lovemaking. Slower. Sensual. Longer. Backwards. Forwards. Sideways. She no longer placed herself over cliff edges. Under water. In space. In every room of wherever they might be. On the floor. Ceiling. Walls. There was at least no longer that need then. Everything was there. In many ways strange. Liking it. But questioning it later. Wanting something else. So when he made movements for her tongue to move in the way he wanted. Knew. The way that gave him pleasure. She still held on to him in stillness.

A resting place.

This way of holding him, as if she would never let go, perhaps swallow him whole, made him question. Made for movements that did not measure her own. Made her draw away. He grew small. Limp. She stiffened, layers of skin beneath froze, then started shaking. He got up. A dark shape against the window. She knew he could see the palm trees circling the square. Leaves quivering, fan like. The bells started ringing. Soon the music came. Loud. Sounding like a funeral march. Something like Elgar. And even before the sun was up she heard the voices of the Totanacs setting up their stalls under the kite-like awnings.

After breakfast, exhausted, they went down into the market. Wandered past those who had perhaps walked from villages many miles away, taking two or three days, laden with wares they hoped to bargain over. Sashes. Shawls. Vegetables. Fruit. Pyramids of oranges. They pushed through the crowds, down the white stone steps, to where a large circle gathered round a 'rainmaker'. In front of him were bottles of liquid, in which appeared to be floating various kinds of twigs, or pieces of bark. Also spread out were large coloured pictures of diseased bodies. One in black and white of a nude woman clutched by a skeleton death figure, behind her, with arms outstretched as if ready to devour her also, a masked surgeon. Meanwhile the 'rainmaker' thumped his chest, shouting to the silent, watchful Indians, that his 'medicine' could cure cancer, bellyache, headaches and alcoholism. He had a small *machete*, which he used with dramatic gestures, pointing at the pictures, the various diseased parts, then bringing the *machete* up, making a slicing gesture a few inches from his naked sweating chest, while his eyes rolled white. The performance must have lasted an hour. She watched the Indians, who intently watched, listened.

Finally when the 'rainmaker' stopped shouting, held the bottles up, many of the Indians passed their five *pesos* over for the 'medicine'. She wondered if he sold 'love' potions.

They walked on through the crowded streets, past stalls with many coloured ribbons, material. They were stared at. Surrounded when they decided to have their feet measured for sandals. The leather felt good, strong, yet light on her feet. But she was aware the women giggled as she walked by. Back in the hotel she took the sandals off. Soon she heard the priest's voice, as if through a microphone, sounding similar to the 'rainmaker's'.

He had gone across to his studio, opposite the hotel. A large empty loft place he had rented with much haggling from a man whose face was covered in carbuncles. Who was always sat outside the doorway. Was his body covered in carbuncles? She shivered. Yet it was hot. Unbearably so. She found a shaded part on the balcony to read. Even reading proved difficult. She found herself looking down at those who came and went, or just squatted outside stores. Beggars who stood silently outside the hotel entrance, and waited until someone from the kitchen brought them something, a *tortilla*, something perhaps they themselves had left at lunchtime. Beggars that were very different from those in the cities. Their eyes alone asking, without demanding.

She looked across to where he sat, she could just see his hands moving forward, backwards over paper. If only. If he would lean more forward. Look up. Out of the window. Come to her now. She looked further down and watched the carpenter opposite, always at work. Painting bright blue coffins with white intricate designs. Small coffins. Sometimes larger. Often he carried one down the street, on his back, supported by the strap around his forehead. At that moment he was carefully painting black shiny crosses, very large, like bedposts. Suddenly she was aware of someone standing behind her. She knew it could not be… she would have recognized his steps. It was the boy who cleaned their room. She smiled, then turned away. He came nearer, leaned on the table. She quickly picked up the book and pretended to read. She knew he watched her, watched without focusing his eyes on her. As if in some trance. He was so close now she could smell his sweat. What did he want? She did not know the Spanish even to say please go, please leave me alone. Did she want to be alone? She was alone. And the boy who cleaned their room, in silence, every day, who slept in a dark alcove downstairs, she felt his loneliness. He leaned nearer. Breathing heavily. She stood up, called out to him across the street. He came to the studio window, she gestured frantically. He shouted to the boy to leave. The boy left muttering '*Gringos Gringos*'.

She went into the room. Lay down. Music. Bells. The priest's voice, or was it the 'rainmaker's' again? Continual hammering of the carpenter. She went out to the balcony and looked over the railings at the huge wooden Quetzal birds. Dozens of them, with white painted eyes. Beaks ready to erect. She walked along to the small chapel, she had not somehow dared to enter before. Confronted again by the Quetzal birds, a dozen at least here faced the altar. Next to the altar a wash basin. She left quickly. And went for a walk. Men stared, whistled, shouted out. Ah, how different when walking with him. She climbed over some rocks, through the maize and crouched in an alcove of orange trees. Remaining there until the sun went down behind the purple, blue mountains, outlined against the sky. Frozen waves. If only it would rain tonight. She walked back, eyes lowered. As the Indian women, the older ones, lowered theirs. And the men leaned against white walls, seeming to laugh. At her. At death, somehow depriving it of any power to wound. A detachment from life. From death.

She remembered one of the many legends about the volcanoes:
Ixtaccihuatl was a lovely princess wooed by Popocatepetl. When he failed to win her, he turned her to stone, and then himself too, so that he might contemplate her forever.

Ixtaccihuatl, the sleeping princess.

As she walked down towards the hotel she heard distant thunder. Wind out of the dust from the high plateau. Through the maize stalks. Perhaps it would rain at last. At last

Rain.

The water-carrier passed her. She could never quite decide whether or not he was a half-wit, or just very drunk on *pulque*. He paused, tossed his head, laughing, and came towards her. The buckets tilted on the pole, water spilling out. She nodded, and walked quickly on. She hoped he would be back in their room, wondering where she had gone. Worried perhaps. At times in the heat of the afternoon she felt almost an urge to go out alone, walk into some part of the jungle, amongst the palm trees, bananas, maize. Give herself to some Indian. Without words. Be ravished. Even raped. Then killed. A quick death from a *machete*. The violence of that afternoon sun. At least now there was the wind sweeping across from the mountains, through the valleys. Stronger. And the thunder nearer. She had a headache. Felt a cat-like restlessness.

He was in the room. Brushing his hair. He did not say anything. But continued brushing, brushing, brushing his hair. She longed for a touch. A word. Something. Later as they lay in bed, she leaned over him. The rain started. Soon heavy rain like tidal waves on the roofs. She took him in her mouth. He moved gently, then faster.

Rain above. Below.

Soon rushing down her throat. Filling her. Filling the area she had so nearly reached.

So it was in moments.

The next day again began with loud music. Bells. The carpenter hammering. Road menders just outside the hotel. The breaking of stones. Two men sifted limestone. Stones laid in a mosaic pattern. They all stopped working as a pig got loose again, was lassoed, led down the street, squealing, struggling back from the rope.

Soon they would leave this town. They had decided. She had decided. He accepted. She would go on ahead. Alone. To New Mexico. He would perhaps join her later. A temporary break. A rest. From the pain that still lingered. The prong of a harpoon catching under the skin. And what would happen, or not happen, she accepted.

She would wait.

But not a waiting between life and death. Arrows and stones. Rather a sitting still on some high rock facing the mesas. So still she would seem a statue. And the lock would be part of her weight. A part of his. A place where they could contemplate each other. From a distance. An area they could meet in. Separate.

Touch in silence.

I'll take the ashes to his wife tomorrow. Idiot. No not again – go away. Never. Get off my back. You're obsessed. I'm not you were. I am. She saw eyes between skin shadows on glass. The full moon that's what it is, nothing else. Move on. Out. Into. Back. Forward. Why can't you just be a memory with the rest. Bottled. Hooded. Closed sequence. I'm still young. You're old, a hag, bitch, spiderwoman. Mean damn you Irish bastard let go.

She fell sideways through trees, rocks, arches, a half open door, between columns. The sea he tossed on. Towards her, white faced, in a wave. Sound of waves breaking up the middle of her head. You killed me finally. Look I'm not responsible, anyway I'm free now. Why do you sit with your legs crossed, wearing the same clothes day in, night out? I'll throw your ashes into the sea would you like that? She saw him rising out. Above her. Above. Below the railway crossing. You were so cold. Still am. You looked like Christ. Ah not the Buddha then? No – Christ. She laughed. What an image. The wigged, satin-robed statue she flew from. The penitents sitting silently, wearing crowns of thorns, scene from The Last

Supper, the large, long wooden table. A high wall she looked over, some nuns singing in the distance. Were you looking for Christ then? Ah God no. A father? No – a brother. No a mother. A lover. It's no use I'm taking you to your wife do you hear and your children tomorrow. Tomorrow how can you presume… in this your darkest hour know that I am with you… her mother's voice with the bagpipes. Oi oi oi.

Her eyes fell back into her head, slits of white, insect flickering. She saw him on the floor under his wife. In music they rose. Fell. In the car with some other woman. Go go go. Get out of this country. Deliver the ashes. Move on. Wings moved from the Kachina doll. Her eyes stopped in mid-flight. She reached for the tranquillisers. Quitter. I must sleep. Must live. Find a life. You've found death. Death on tracks, weeds, flowers between elbows. How many times did I fall asleep while you went on and ononononon. Through others, past those who finally didn't care, couldn't take it. Take you. Take me with you take me out of this country where I no longer belong. What country belongs now to anyone? Revolution. A new religion. Prophet of the Aquarian Age will you please… You persist in going through words damn you when

Enclosed form. The shell moved in circles. Movement of candle flame against white walls. Her head rested against sand, a jet seat, grass, water. One tree. A wood with orange mushrooms. She had wanted to understand the language of birds. They spoke now get out getoutgetoutget. She moved to a corner of the room and waited until he finished making love. Listened to their breathing. Moans. What cries then. I did outside. A marriage. Waiting. You never waited for anything. Oh God shutup. Never. You tried being God wanting things to happen. They happened. Hand raised she watched the candle go out. That's it. But without you? I'm here. Go away. Her shadow tossed over curtains. As simple as that. Who cares?

No one. None of the others. Victims. Am I a victim too? That's up to you. You're dead do you hear absolutely totally annihilated. What do you want to prove? I should have taken out your heart. And held it to the sun? She leaned over the shell, breathed in the sea dust. Long fibres. Hair, skin, ears to hold. Holding her body between elbows. Crouching. Listen. I can't. Won't. Wouldn't. I hear too much. No more. Silence. There is no silence hear the blood humming. Brainwires. Fire. No silence in the beginning. Remember the numbness. I didn't hear I saw. Illusion. Thought forms. All in the mind. I saw only what you saw. I see now through your eyes, ears, bones, mouth. The taste of some afternoon woman. The ones we shared. How many of those? Does that matter? How many do you remember? The third. I was always that. Outside. A voyeur never – you enjoyed it as much as… stop. Her hands came up. She looked at the bone structure, veins, a Chinese watercolour she wanted to wipe out.

Begin again. Move on. Move back. Move into gestures familiar. Her mother sewing. Gathering sweetpeas. No

man about the house. Walls of old ladies. Dutch oil paintings. Mousetraps, mothballs, lavender letters. Candlewax.
Icicles. Crash of chamberpots. Voices picked up. Listen.
I hear nothing they've all pushed up the daisies. They
are here. Here today there tomorrow. Listen

Thud of small bodies on glass. Window held the room.
Rooms she followed him in. Left no part of himself.
Left her to clear up the remains. Ash. Red candlewax
dripped on to layers of skin peeled off. Coldness of a
gun. Warmth of rocks in the dark. Where he had slept.
Passed out the night before. Killing the day. A country
he left but bringing it in his eyes. Blue Irish. I've seen
the devil and he's not a leprechaun. Yes you said that
lying in a cave. I wasn't lying.

The cave she wanted to enter. With him. Move with
him. Wherever. Whatever. Always a step ahead. Faster
than the sounds she picked up. Faster than the things she
threw at him. Words, moods, silences, doors he closed
behind her. Opened. Left her to open. Close. Knock down.
Pull apart. Areas run through she lingered in. Places
paused in now thrust aside.

A place. No placing. No placement. Objects picked up.
Dropped. A pen, letters, books, photos of his mother,
dad, brothers, sisters, wives, loves, friends. Faces looked
up at her. Family groupings with the taste of porridge
on their smiling mouths. Still lives wondering about
him. His wanderings. Scribbled notes pleading money
for his kids. Asking for the ashes. All of them. Not one
piece must I keep. No don't tear her up. Yes. You bitch.

You never loved that one. I loved them all for their love at the time. You don't know what love is. Illusion. Shit. When the Saints Come Marching In. When Irish Eyes are smiling… Stop.

She lit a cigarette. Flame caught a strand of hair. She scratched the dry bits away. Pieces of faces. Out of the wood. No you're not out of it. Not yet I know that. Spaces he made for her to fill in. A space between walls, clouds, stars, mountains. Feet placed at angles to form the earth as she held on. Nothing to hold on to. No one. That's it indulge in self-pity. Go on. Go where? I am here. There. Where are you? She lit a candle. Now will you stop? I never stop. She hissed. Closed her eyes. If only he would stop. Never. What do you want what is it wanted now. Now?

Wind blew the curtains sideways. Lifted the Indian rug suspended from wooden beams. Wind across her feet. Face. Across his. As they lay on the mesa between rocks. The desert under his arms. She watched rain in the distance. Curtains of rain moving slowly. Wanting to watch that. So much time spent in a country where hearing it meant just another day of bloody weather. And voices commenting cold today yes but not as cold as yesterday looks like rain. Could I return to that? Yes once this assignment is over. The papers are signed. The death certificate. Everything is in order. I'll get a ride tomorrow. Someone must be leaving town. If not then the time is not right. Is it ever right? Let things happen.

Slide, fall back, into a rose garden. Do such places still exist? The sound of tea cups on a Sunday. The steady mower rhythm. Newspapers. Walks in parks. Drizzle. Grey buildings. Toll of church bells. Backyards of machinery. Did they still hang out the washing on Mondays? Yes. Of course. That distance. How many hours forward? Time. No time. No sense of yesterday. What happened a week ago. Not then. Flying from place to place. Corners. No spaces now for filling in. Leap away and they're there. Waiting. Watching. If yer don't watch out the Goblins will git yer. They got you all right in the end. I knew they would. They're there all the bugs circling circling. Dried white skin. You looked so pale. Thanks for not letting the worms get me. Oh let me rest, let me think, let me dream, let me alone. You are alone. Damn you Goddamn you – no no don't leave me. The door swung back she saw him kneeling between legs. Knew what the next move would be. Counter-movement. Anticipation. You were a rotten lousy lover did ever anyone tell you that? You kept coming I made you come hours after. Make me now. She spread out her legs. Felt the heat of fire. No Dairymaid Your Search Has Ended. Somewhere in a small town licking icecream. He rolled joints in one hand, drove with the other, chatted up three chicks in the back seat. Their faces stretched on bone racks. Teeth rattled in the back of her head. Something pulled down her neck. Just under hair. Hold me. Hold the tears that can't come. You cried enough when

Yes in the dark. A banshee wailing. Flies on your face. Flies' blood on yellow paper. Strips of yellow they stuck to in the kitchen. Curtains of them. Of white hair a mad old lady in her room brushed the days out. Perhaps I'll end up like her. Well at least that would be a quiet madness. She threw a log on to the fire. It fell to the side. See. Listen. Branches against windows, walls, faces, eyes peering in. Out out. Out all of you. She swept the air around. Wood caught fire in a tunnel. A cave. Sound of a gun going off. She saw apricots falling. No sound. Noise of shells rotating. Seasons of landscapes moved round in frames. England. America. Mexico.

Where are you now? A stretch of beach under white cliffs. Green smoothed edges. A river holding, letting go branches. You were plumper then. Yes. Young, young, intense. And you were… Ah. Full of revolutions, ideals. Freaking out in a more dispersed way. Here's a photo of you. Get rid of that. College kid, quick tyre changer that's all nothing else all in the mind, stars didn't change their course, cars didn't levitate, you can't kid me, not now. She scratched a mosquito bite. Drew blood. She wanted not to see that. The blood. In the palm of her hand. But there was no blood. Not a stain on the track. Only flattened weeds. Sound of crickets. A drum in the distance that went on all day. Firecrackers, a Ferris wheel. And bodies moved round a body stretched out. Was there a bottle in the hand, Tequila, Whisky? Something. A slight mark on the right side of the mouth. No the left side. Coffee. A bruise. Jesus I don't know. A shadow dropping into the others. Let it fall quietly. But there's always something stirring under leaves. Foxes moving with the light. Edge of afternoon. Evening. Yes with

No. Not that. She moved over the side of the bed. On her belly, legs together. Spread. Over his shoulders. His tongue rotated fast in her. Make me big again. In the saying of it he was there. Demon-riding his body attached to hers. Demons rushed into her. Filling the hours spent waiting. Watching. Nourishing herself. On what? Interpretation misinterpreted. No time. No space for recapitulation. The days. Events. A wheel that never stopped rolling down from the edge. The sides. Front. The back. All parts taken into account. Dismissed. Go on. Unnecessary. Everything is necessary. In the description. It happened. What is happening now? Nothing.

Throw away those dead flowers. Light a candle, some incense. Move about. Move on. Move inward. Let me feel you move inside me. Standing up. Suspended. No sense of gravity. Move move move. I can't. She clutched her knees, throat, his back, his dreams. Fantasies. Were there any left? Yes undressing her while she climbed the stairs, a style. Tied to a bed and raped. You never would. Wanted to, often thought of it at times you know when I thought that. Do you have fantasies now – are you there?

Some creature bumped against the outside wall. Moist fur in a crack. Let me rest in you. Sleep while in you. Sleep. Ach sleep is for the birds. Listen. The bells. All the bells ringing. Ding dong and pussy's… Must be Sunday. They'll be thronging the plaza in their best. Stalls of sizzling meat crawling with flies and buzzards over-head. Waiting. And back home yes still 'home' they'll be having a TV newspaper vegetated day. Walking after their dogs in parks; thin men with thin growls dreaming of muzzling their fat wives. 'Timber,' a purple woman shouts 'come here,' and there's a crashing through the trees, behind the trees a strip of steel that is a lake, and beyond a tower of light, a rocket. You sound nostalgic. No – shit – the only thing to do there is to spend it in bed. An orgy. Yes yes. Yes. Orgy of roast beef and Yorkshire pud. Ah! Missed that cup of tea, just the words have a cup of nice tea dear the kettle's boiling won't take a minute you'll feel better. Safe comfortable rituals, the monotony that keeps the fantasies moving. Do you still fantasise about killing your father? Chop him up into little pieces – yes why not I'm playing at sanity anyway. Ah you think you're mad – never. Neither sane or insane – the thin edge I tread and I want to go over. And end up like me – yes perhaps it would be an experi-ence for you that's what you want EXPERIENCE in caps period. To live beyond myself. Such a craving. Ashes into ashes. Never marked on the middle of the forehead. Ash Wednesday. Envied those who could. You have the chance now. Sackcloth. The lot. Yes. Haven't washed for days. When was the last time hands felt water. The sun in a wave. High waves tossed her under. He rode out. Sea at night an express train over rocks. Part of dreams. You weren't fucking me then could have been anyone. That's right I was fucking mermaids. Your wife. Wives.

All the beautiful women I saw didn't see. They saw what a bastard you were. All dying to save me save the image. So many. Images. The roles were a drag. What did you want what was wanted – what wanted of me now? Carry on, do what you have to do. Deliver the ashes and then? Make things happen you have the power. Without you? I'm with you. Is it your power, is it your face, eyes, voice without your body. Look those eyes between stems looking in. Always looking in. Seeing too much. Hearing too much. How can I go on? Words with double intentions. Objects with triple signs. Nothing is as simple as it was. Mind-blown. Ghostworm riddled. Listen. What do you hear? Mermaids, drums, soft bodies falling, a train carrying the night across the border.

Tomorrow or in two, three days I will cross that border, the papers are ready. She climbed out of curled back against wall. Groped under the bed. Yes they're still there. Her fingers covered in dust crawled out. Guard them careful now they might jump out hit you in the face. Cover my body in your ashes. Yes I want you to hurt me so I might feel something. I want to feel my body again it's a vehicle moving the weight I no longer feel. She threw off her clothes. She passed her hands over the mirror. Then pressed against it. Hair hung down over her face. Just a body moving. Sitting. Standing. Look though it dances yes it can still dance. She swayed back, arms out as if to gather in the room. Look. She puppet-gestured. Bent and snatched up the vase. Ashes scattered, rolled under the bed. Look you can dance too or are you laughing? Cool it. Not this time you can't stop me now. She leaped on to chairs, table, bed. Ashes rolled at her feet. Suppose I never stop. Dance into death, dancing with it. For it. Listen to the blood humming backwards. Forwards. One, two, three. Are you one or two? Duality divided. I love you. She kissed her reflection. Lips pressed on ice. All over skin changing. Nipples erect, eyes bright. Take that grin off. There wipe it out. Soft smile pout. Oh yeah you were always a good actress. Balls. Turning everything into soap opera. I didn't have to with you around. She finger signed her eyes. Slanted. Time for a change. You changed me. No – no one changes no one. Maybe I ought to be a kept woman don't you think it's about time someone looked after me. Me damn you. Let go. She threw up her arms and curled her feet away from the ashes. From you see. Witch. Motherfucking monster. A log thudded down from the centre of the fire. OK I'm sorry. Kiss my feet, then kneel down, lick my toes. She sank to the floor. Head buried between her knees. Do you remember the eclipse? The slow darkness moving over an orange moon. Nights after the eclipse. The first light passing across skin. Skin felt new then. Layers shed from English winters. Bedsitters, city boxes, subway ovens. Marching feet. Assassinations. A closed off room with all the bells… Those goddamn bells. She shall have rings on her fingers and bells on her…

Wherever she doesn't go. At least I won't end up like you no doubt staggering over the railway crossing, shouting out, cursing the world, cursing your mother, that endless dialogue marked by manic flights of fancy. You weren't there. I heard I knew before it happened. Exercise other body areas as well. Exorcise did you say?   ?   What? Stop grinning your wife won't be when I give her those ashes. How do you know they're not all laughing their fucking heads off right now yeah it'll be agreed we knew he'd come to a bad end he had to pay the price and so on in their utopian bliss of hygiene and economics. Let's change the subject. Deep down he had a tender heart, however, and never killed women or children, or tourists out of season, he never scalped his victims; he was too civilised for that, he used to skin them gently and tan their hides. Oh you're too much. I suppose as usual you think I'm on a Rip Van Winkle kick — you always thought I couldn't keep up with you well at first I couldn't. Didn't want to. I was dumb, a dumb broad being taken for a ride, a ride that took over. You weren't dumb for long. Numb. Hypnotised I just wanted to watch, follow.

She followed him into parties. Out. Followed even when she remained behind. Now he will miss me. But he didn't. Didn't return. She found him rapping always rapping to someone and if no one then to himself. Or screwing someone's wife. Even that I got used to after a while. Oh never it's against your puritanical upbringing. I had to get used to it. Well I never got used to those women so ready so willing to be laid for the sacrifice. Some of them didn't have anything better to do. Ah! Oh leave me let me sleep tonight I'm cold my feet are so cold. She stretched out in front of the fire. Let me rest. No time for that. Yes. You have a lot to learn. Haven't I learned enough more than anyone living should know? Excuse me ma'am there's much more to learn. I can't go on. Listen – watch – watch now everything watches senses things just as they happen often before they happen. I knew you would die. That was without doubt. Die the way you did alone. I wouldn't have chosen it otherwise. If only...

If she had gone by instinct that night. All those nights. Seen the signs. What use now? I want to recapitulate, gather in the threads. Leave it for them to do, the fuzz, jerks like that take the notes have them recorded, what do you want to imitate? A history. One man's history aie. Find the clues. They're around you, in you, with you. Yes you are. You want to be objective, see how things tie up, the cause and effect all so Freudian, memory psychological shit. Oh go to hell. I've been. Just leave me I want to reconstruct. She raised her hands to the fire. Raised her face to his. Facing the rain in an orange grove. The avoidance of it in England, the umbrella life. How can that country hold anything for me now? Squared off fields. Cabbage patches. Clipped hedges. Axe-happy gardeners. Clipped voices. Don't forget the bluebells. Yes they can call. Cuckoo. Well allow me something out of that country. Safe little island that's going to sink into the channel any minute with Her Majesty reading out Rule Britannia we shall never be slaves – how does it go? Ask me another. And this country with its rituals, death, the smell of death in earth, I can still smell your body, the sweat on your clothes and… If salt is put on a snail it is annihilated. Did you do that? Yes I can see you as a kid deliberately slowly pouring salt over the poor creature. Curiosity. That carried you through a lot. The plot thickens. I'm tired let me just think. Think you never stop – shoot first think afterwards. Your motto. My life. Your death. Where's your Private Investigator badge of Solid Bronze for lifetime wear? I'm turning in. Turn over.

Yes I can begin again once I've… You're on the out-side looking in. You dragged me in. Yes by the hair and you loved it don't tell me otherwise. Oh not that violence. He snarled as she lifted her hand. Hands held, head hit, body knocked. Head thrust against the wall. Goddammit I'll kill you. He shouted. Go ahead kill me then anything anything but… She felt the wall several times as he banged her head against it. The violence at such times amazed her. Wanting that when they made love. Forcing it on him hurt me hurt me. And he tried. Afterward she wanted more. Wanted him to want but he slept. When he wanted she longed to talk. When she talked he insisted on something else. Some happening. Something always had to happen. Sensationalist. Speak for yourself. Learn when to say yes. No. Yes to life. Yes to death. Yes to love as it happens and yes when it doesn't. I inhabit the hearts of old women, the kind with paper bags, crumbs for the pigeons, or with the froth of beer on over-red lips, crouched in a pub corner whispering to herself, or to a stiff-legged dog. Ah yes a witch with her familiar.

This witch then is getting out of town right away deliver the ashes – where are they? She crawled along, picked up the ashes one by one. There in you go. Best to put a lid on I might crawl out and roll into your dreams. Maybe they aren't... Yes of course they are whose do you think they might be? Well like sometimes... Drop them and see careful one by one listen who would make that much noise. She held the vase to her head. What in heaven's name are you chuckling about now? I'm not I'm dancing. Are you stoned again I mean... No just stones rolling them around good for divining you know. Divine my dreams tonight. It's morning look. I don't want to. She looked at the play of light in three frames reflected on the wall. Seascapes. Landscapes. Townscapes. Held in memory. Focused. A couple walking. Bending under apple trees. A woman stretched out naked between pillars. Is she dead – myself? No look she turns over and faces the pillars. Pillars of snow rising out of still water. A half open door on a stretch of sand. Fade out.

Move to the window. Look already the beggars are putting on their faces, their bodies for the tourists. You can be cruel you know. Not cruel enough. What is enough I shall never know. Enough is more than less. Enough then I'll pack some things, leave right away. Don't forget your shadow. Oh yes that goes first.

She collapsed on the bed. Blankets over her face. You'll suffocate. I am already. For what? Sleep. The bed a boat she struggled from edge to edge. Light filled half the room, spaces between cracks, leaves, faces. Sound of feet, sandalled, naked feet passed by. The whine of a mosquito. She curled up, hardly able to breathe, bathed in sweat. She emerged from the sea, grass, rocks, rooms. Lovers she hardly knew. Hardly knew herself then. Anonymous. Picked up at a party. Some talked. Others preferred not to. But inevitably that silence in the morning. Exchange of 'phone numbers thrown away later. How many? What matter now we've gone over it all before countless times. Numberless. Of course – look damn you go away. No I want to hear more. More of what? Those who entered before me. Entries, exits and that was all. Must have been some who… What about yourself then? You… Look I want to sleep you realise I haven't for three days. That's nothing besides you'll be able to hallucinate, have better trips, the mind gets clogged with sleep, obvious dreams. A need to dream I shall go mad otherwise, perhaps I am already – am I mad? Don't you want to be? Don't you ever get tired? No just exhausted by all this shit. If it's such a drag go somewhere else haunt your wife or some other chick there must be someone who… No curiosity makes me stay. Ah yes I have the remains I suppose as long as I have these with me there's no possibility… I shall still be with you. Why me why? It's your choice. Am I choosing then to be mad, I don't even know what day it is, how long I've been here, may as well be in an isolation ward, don't need a strait jacket my body is that, those beggars will enter one day and I won't say a word, they'll pick my bones, yes I can hear them quarrelling over those, throwing my remains around. If you want that to happen… Tell me what can happen what can I make happen now? Go with from moment to moment. And this assignment? Which one? You know very well – you have promised yourself. Yes I suppose so. No time to lose. I'm losing my patience I'm going. Good. She turned over, face buried in the pillow. Foot against foot. Knee against knee. She turned over on her back and stared at the ceiling. The rug swayed slightly. Are you still there? She whispered, then laughed as the rug jerked. You said you were going. I decided to come back. Is it lonely out there wherever is it? Too crowded. Bring someone in then let's have a party, turn on. Days being turned on, days into nights, no longer knowing the separation of dark from light. You have gone haven't you? She shouted out. Who is it here who's taken your place tell me who are you? Keep cool I'm here all right. Prove it. Always proof needed! Give me a sign, prove it here, prove it now. She looked round the room. Things picked up from other places. Areas reminded of. So many useless things. Countless shells. Numberless feathers. Beads, drawings, records, books. I shall leave them all behind and start a new life, without belongings, nothing familiar, collect only people's thoughts. What an ambition! That's what you wanted. Do you really think you can inhabit me? I am inhabited. Then I shall leave. She made a sign and laughed. Ah so you still want to inhabit me you wanted to while you lived – are you there – gone – good then I can dream. Dream back. Into. Forward. Scenes not comprehended at the time. Can they be comprehended now? How can I be sure what I conjure up won't be misinterpreted? He's really gone, no answer, no mocking retort. Peace. Oh God. No, steady, keep cool, yes that's it loosen the back of the neck. Eyes closed. See further than what's in front of your nose. Hear with the eyes, see with the ears. Listen

Time back. Above oceans. Out of reach. In touch with glass, clouds, islands of vapour. The thought of death occurred as usual when in the air, not fear, but a wallowing in the thought of plummeting like a bird through space. Body accelerating at 32 feet per second, falling at approximately 120 miles per hour. The plane landed safely between wing shadows.

City at noon, hot, crowded. Steel and concrete removed the light. Columns of darkness she stepped out of into a darker place. A corridor. A smaller corridor. A bed, washbasin, cold water, wardrobe. Clanging of hangers bent from many hands, many shapes. She locked the door. Could not open the window, thick with dust. Thick with the noise from traffic. She lay on the bed, in her coat, on wheels and roots of trees. She woke up hot, exhausted, hungry. She ordered something, anything, reminder of an English breakfast. Someone in uniform entered, and though they spoke the same language, she knew she was a foreigner, and so did he taking the dollars out of her shaking hand, leaving a smell of soap and burnt toast. Waves of traffic through the blinds. Opposite were gaps of light. Arrows. Disks revolving. Static. There was no sky.

Many sounds. Police sirens throughout the night. Televisions. Wind rattled the blinds, window. She wrote letters, tore them up and like a spy flushed them away. She attempted reading, flung the book down and emerged into humid air. Walked quickly round several blocks, looking as if she had somewhere to go, someone to meet. Startled by doorways holding shapes, taking on human form only after she had passed. Surprised by animals in cages on the edge of a park. The edge of a sidewalk. Rubber and asphalt. A slight wind. Hot. Dust and newspapers. Was that the moon or not. Plastic. Neon stars. Narrow frames of darkness. Solitary man walked with white poodles. Others in groups. Others huddled over bars. Women stepped into yellow cabs, yellow faces squeezed on dry bones. Laughter with the edge of hysteria. And the howling of police cars, ambulances.

Revolving doors of glass. Fingers curled round the key to a room she did not want to enter. Over a bed that faced the door. She faced the wall and closed her eyes. Sat up, smoked. Picked up the telephone, put it back – supposing his wife answered – sorry wrong number or OK this is it if he hasn't told you well… She checked her watch, money, travellers' cheques, passport, visa. Everything in order. Could she order sleep, someone to talk to, a return ticket. No the decision had been made. Things would change.

The light changed, filtered in through the blinds. A faint blue rubbed the walls. She did not know where she was. Extending this, extending the bed, the room. The other side of walls a garden. Walled in green. In this she went back to sleep. Waking several hours later she picked up the phone. He answered, sleepy, distant, not surprised, inviting her to come out to New Mexico, yes he had told his wife, she knew about it all, his meeting with her in England, yes there had been rows of course but ah well… When would she like to come – oh now she said laughing, breathless, caught her face in the mirror, an overblown middleaged woman, and only a year had passed since their last coming together on her narrow bed that had somehow miraculously widened during their brief relationship. In a week, she said, a week's time I'll be there. And relented as soon as the phone wires hummed. What could she possibly do by herself in an alien city – a whole week, remain in the room, cause suspicion, let herself be picked up, well why not, easier than a woman on her own. She no longer felt the independence that London gave her. Like a child whimpering, and nearly falling off the stool when waiters shouted Yeah wotcherwant, she heard her English schoolgirl voice, a caricature, answer black coffee please, while all around carefully shaved faces pressed against hamburgers and four-tiered sandwiches. Only a midget looked at her, she became absorbed by the bubbles in the coffee, not black, but 'regular' she did not dare to point it out to the waiter who muttered under his breath. She watched the thick drops of ketchup fall in ominous lumps on someone's hamburger, and she shuddered. She looked quickly away and caught the midget's eyes, blackcurrants in a sponge, he leaned over, English – yeah thought so – Stan's the name, wrestler by profession – was in Manchester during the blitz – but you're not from there right?

In a daze she went from bar to bar with Stan, his wiry wrestler hand clutched her arm. But he made her laugh, relax, and she found herself talking over bourbons with 'a little whaterr', until his face ballooned, shrivelled, then there were two midgets beside her rocking backwards, forwards, and she saw herself the fat lady in a circus. She tottered to the rest room, no graphite here, oh not like London, Victoria Station, Piccadilly, no grey haired attendant outside knitting, no notices about V.D. perhaps they called it something else here. She staggered out towards a little wrestler who wrestled with a long cigarette and a Manhattan on the rocks. She mentioned New Mexico, you'll get scalped there, he shrieked, or – and passed a hairy finger across his hairier neck.

They ended up downtown in some bar where he was known. This is Belle she's a wrestler too. She shook hands with a huge blonde woman who never spoke but laughed, whose eyes seemed to have no pupils, and teeth that looked as if they would fall out any moment, they did a moment later landing in her rum and coke, some obscene pink monster floating to be picked up and popped into a whale's mouth, that closed but immediately opened wide revealing a wrinkled tongue rolled over itself. They were invited back to Belle's apartment, full of fur it seemed, or were there that many cats. Walls lined with photographs of women wrestling in mud. She fell asleep on a fur settee and woke up to the sound of milk cans, grunts, moans and cats meowing. Through a half open door she saw the two wrestlers thumping it out.

She found herself in a narrow street lined with dust-bins, bottles, dogs, cats and what looked like bundles of old clothing, which moved when she passed, and she saw white bony hands clasp a bottle, another a syringe. Where on earth was she, oh God, and there was a cop with baton swinging gun holstered at the end of the street. She quickly turned and half ran back the way she had come. She entered a subway, silently screaming in the inferno, this she felt would be a recurring nightmare, almost as if she had already dreamed it, but would there be the relief of waking up? Any moment she felt she'd throw a fit, or lose consciousness, the thought of those stuffed animals coming alive to trample on her body gave her some strength. Lines of robots behind newspapers, eggy mouthcorners, the smell of dirty sheets, toothpaste and four day control. Women with restless nights still in their glazed eyes, all freshly madeup but already powder cracking in the heat. Mouths masticating chewing gum, one side of jaw working furiously. She'd heard of grim things going on in the subway. Any moment a knife would be plunged into her back. Sickly bespectacled youth opposite her, his eyes on her legs, and yet further up, moved his hand in his trouser pocket. She uncrossed her legs, but crossed them again, tried to pull her skirt down. His hand moved more quickly. She got out. Was he going to follow? Her heart moved with her clicking heels, was that panting behind her? In broad daylight who would have thought but rapists would live in their own time. She arrived outside and became anonymous in the crowd surging up Fifth Avenue.

She entered a gaudy restaurant, all brass, chrome and mirrors. Eggs and bacon she said in a loud voice, the waitress yawned sunnyside up? Yes. That sounded good, like daffodils, or wheatfields, and she could almost smell a harvest, see the cornflowers, poppies above her head, and larks rising, rising into expanse of blue. The twisting path through the longer grass, her favourite walk until one day horror, she saw the white stick first, then legs with stockings rolled down waving in the air. Well of course blind men were men after all and… She never took the same walk again.

Twin suns surrounded by withered earwigs lay on a plate before her, she pierced one sun and watched it explode over the earwigs. A man with three chins, or was the third his collar, spread out opposite, he barricaded himself with the Wall Street Journal. She gulped some coffee down, paid and left. Left for what? There were always museums.

She felt dizzy in the Guggenheim, squares, dots of colour rose and fell, fell and rose. Oh for the stillness of the Turner Gallery, and the nodding keepers, the licking lapping Thames after a rather nasty cup of tea, and the bit of park near the Houses of Parliament, the solid oh so solid statues reminding that one lived in a history.

She caught a cab back to the hotel, the driver delighted to find she was English, his wife was, and out came photos of his family, all effigies of himself, six kids from the Bronx, but one in Vietnam now a good strong lad ma'am fighting for our country – those dirty yellow bastards. She told him to stop, even though it wasn't anywhere near the hotel. And though hot, exhausted she walked in a park and saw a wider margin of sky.

Later back at the hotel she phoned. I'm coming out there tomorrow OK? She heard the sounds of jazz behind his stoned voice, and he talked non-stop, the line crackled, a shrill operator's voice came on, or was it his wife? Then his mumbling, followed by shouting I said I want to fuck you front and back you bitch in a London telephone box and let 'em all see what a fine ass you have ma'am and bounce your lovely big tits up and down and get ten year old to gangbang you under Nelson's column... hey... what time will you... OK right I'll meet you at the station and morning glory seeds to push up your – what can't hear where the hell are you – look if you're lonely phone up a friend of – man – ho what a lovely man here's the number – motherfucking kids shutup will you I'm talking to an English lady – Goddammit the Queen of England fuck off. She wrote the number down, screwed it up, searched for it later when darkness came. I'm a friend of... where are you now baby well why dontcher you come on down pick up a cab.

She arrived at a warehouse, an unlit street. A large studio with three men stoned out of their minds swaying between huge twisted parts of cars painted red and yellow. A real English rose just walk around baby that's it like to see you just walk. They passed reefers around, but didn't offer any to her. She asked for a glass of water, motioned into a partitioned off kitchen where a girl sat feeding a baby, who stared through her and said green parrots dancing on Buddha's arms.

MOTHERLOGUE

Oh hello darling how lovely to hear you thank you for calling on this day   yes I know I know one shouldn't but still we share this don't we dear his death of course it's really his birthday   Well how are things anything happening it's been cold here are you warm enough in that flat I told you how cold it would get   the snow's coming through my kitchen window   no no it's all right now I've stuffed newspaper in it   mmmmmm is it well I haven't been out today are you using the electric blanket I gave you because if not you could bring it back next time you come down all it needs is a longer lead I'm sure Richard can fix that has he done it yet   I see well if you aren't using it I may as well have it back   By the way I've got a new lodger Mr. Mole his name yes really Mole funny isn't it and he's just like one too well he hasn't changed a thing in the room left the furniture exactly as I had arranged it not like some people the only trouble is he will use the lavatory late at night wakes me up and you know the plug being pulled sounds like a deluge coming down and then guess what yesterday he came knocking at my door all white faced said a pigeon had fallen down his chimney and would I see to it he was in a terrible state he'd already moved his bed out and put it in that small kitchen where he went off to while I was left to deal with the pigeon well I called the chimney sweep what a todo and he hasn't moved back in there   no dear the lodger the pigeon was taken out and there he is sleeps in that window-less room with the electric light burning all the time of course I'll have to speak to him I mean the electricity bill is large enough without   yes dear well he's a computer you know works with machines

no he doesn't seem to have a girlfriend

no I don't think he's one of those   what what I can't hear you oh dear this line's terrible can you hear me   oh did you dear well what had your father got to say for himself then   yes he seems a little better walks more quickly seems more coherent doesn't he but he's now got this trouble in his ear like a little heart beating away in there he said and you know what he thinks some insect might have got in there   yes dear an insect in his ear it was certainly on his mind the whole day he came down here he couldn't talk about anything else and you know something every time he visits me he nestles down in the armchair and says oh it's so good to be home again I have the feeling if given half the chance he'd hang his hat up here and oh dear you know how soft I can be and then he tries to kiss me when he leaves but I always turn my cheek the other way   what was that   oh really well I don't know dear I was thinking of flying to Edinburgh for Christmas there's a hotel advertised all in and you and Richard won't want me around you'll want to be together won't you dear and I do have a week off   yes yes well I thought it might be fun go off on my own   well your father told me when he asked what you might be doing for Christmas you said you didn't really know   by the way he asked me when you might get married do you really think   hello hello   are you there who who who's she   oh Richard's wife yes of course well I suppose he must miss the children and that is a problem isn't it dear do you really think she'll divorce him I mean

and oh by the way you might tell him to get that magazine readdressed it keeps coming here you know with his wife's name on it I don't know what the postman must think and sometimes it goes upstairs by mistake and there's a huge parcel for him too he owes me some postage on it I don't know sometimes I feel it's like a post office here   no no dear it doesn't matter it's only a few bob but you know it's unlucky for stamps not to be paid for anyway if he's expecting anything from New York he might not get it the main post office there was burnt down and all the mail for Europe well at least for Britain was completely destroyed   How's Ronnie have you seen him lately do give him my love lovely boy so gentle and understanding   oh you had him round then what did you cook   ah you must tell me the secret of doing that   no no darling I was only kidding of course Richard likes his food doesn't he takes a lot to

feed a man like that of course he needs it all that energy
does he still like his babyfood   milk dear I mean and
he's always eating isn't he still they say it's good to eat
often and little does he still eat with his knife well dear
that time he used the knife with the cheese I mean it
was such a sharp knife he'll cut his tongue one of these
days   Well how are you feeling you sound a bit down
oh yes the weather has been awful did you see in the
paper that poor old woman found frozen to death and
oh my goodness you remember Peggy I forgot to tell
you I saw Lilly at the theatre the other night and she
told me she was earth bound   what dear   no no
not Lilly you know Peggy who was found dead after a
whole week the landlady discovered her only because
of the smell coming out on to the landing there she was
a whole week rotting away well apparently she's earth
bound they've had several new lodgers in and each one
hasn't stayed long terrible things happening in the night
bedclothes taken off furniture thrown about and one girl
even had her nightie torn off   yes yes dear they've
seen her of course it was all Peggy's furniture I bet she's
mad being left there like that for a whole week cheer-
ful soul really wasn't she so full of life terrible thing to
happen you never know do you   Oh by the way dear I
thought perhaps you'd like to come down this weekend
there's a good play on and I could book tickets oh I see
well enjoy yourselves   Oh I forgot to tell you I've
ordered a nice leather bag for you to match your coat
after all that one you've got looks so tatty   How's the

smoking dear I can hear you coughing away you ought to try those small cigars I told you about are you taking those vitamin pills I'm sure Richard is he knows how to take good care of himself   did you read all that about the birth pills of course it might be those that spoil your complexion used to be so nice and clear well it does look kind of dry these days and you look so grey when you do come down I don't think cities really agree with you still God knows where you'll be this time next year the other end of the world I suppose What are you doing for New Year's Eve   oh I see   no no I haven't arranged anything and I'm certainly not going to the Scottish do so cliquish besides they'd only put me next to a terrible old blind man like last time no one else would and they think ah there's old muggins we'll put her next to him as she hasn't got anyone and he's not half as blind as he's supposed to be there he is eyeing all the girls no I'm not putting up with that rather spend it on my own the only problem is I haven't got a first footer   you know dear a dark man to come into the flat after midnight   no no the lodger won't do he's blonde at least I think he is he hasn't got that much hair but I know he's not dark ah well   How's the money side of things have you worked it out between you I mean you can spend a lot of money on food alone feeding a big man like Richard it's a shame he can't get a job   no no not so much the money dear even a voluntary job would get him out of the flat for a while I mean he's really so restless isn't he all that excess energy and besides no woman can stand having a man around all day

    I see well it is difficult to make ends meet for me but then something always turns up even when I'm down to my last penny something turns up my guardian angel looks after me just as well I suppose no one else will I thought I might take up typing lessons can't afford a typewriter though   well next year as you know dear I retire of course everyone is amazed that I've nearly reached retirement age   what what do you mean dear 1/3d for the cinema   oh old age pensioners yes I know it's silly really but when I see these old women drawing their pensions out I think oh dear next year I'll be one of those   yes I know dear still at my age what man will look at me they go after all these young girls not that I really need a man around you know I couldn't bear the idea of sharing the same bed besides I snore no what I want is a nice cultured man just for a companion go to the theatre with occasionally someone who likes classical music and good books but men of my age they're so dull and the ones who do look at me aren't worth a second look   yes well I did go out once with that one but he had such a terrible speaking voice I couldn't bear it besides I think he thought I was a rich widow oh I soon tell them I have a job and the car's not mine but belongs to the firm you soon know then what they're after By the way dear I forgot to mention you know that awful man who came up behind you on the beach and exposed himself well the police have caught a man who's assaulted three women along that stretch of the underwalk I bet it's the same man terrible isn't it you can't go anywhere nowadays rape murder robbery only the other day a poor old woman was coshed to death by hooligans in the grocery just round the corner fancy doing that to a poor defenceless woman   And oh did I tell you about the car gave me a nasty turn the other day this car in front of me a woman driver too which is unusual turned off to the right suddenly no signals nothing good job I had my wits about me and there was a lorry right behind me he had to go up on the pavement don't know what would have happened if he   what dear   oh sorry I always do get a bit shouty when I'm hysterical well it did shake me up   no no the car's all right   Oh I forgot to tell you such an awful dream I had the other night   no dear not the lavatory one wasn't that a strange one there you were hanging half way out of the cistern with all those people looking on and you said you wanted to do it alone that you had to prove something and I thought why demonstrate it in such a difficult way no this dream was really awful I even woke up crying I was searching for you in large buildings then in a huge forest and I couldn't find you anywhere I woke up in a terrible state and it still haunts me funny how some dreams have that effect on one isn't it that one you had of me burning myself like a Buddhist nun   no no I never really try to interpret my dreams just as well probably those nightmare ones amaze me because they always seem to be some kind of prophesy it might take a few months but as sure as fate something linked to the dream happens very weird isn't it   well dear I better ring off this must be costing you something you'll be down on the Sunday I suppose   oh but darling you can't possibly come down on Christmas Day there aren't any trains running   no no nothing that day had you forgotten this is England not America everything closes down here   yes yes I'm absolutely sure anyway I expected you to be down on Christmas Eve I'd like to see something of   OK dear and there's only about one train on Boxing Day so you'll have to go back the following day what's Ronnie doing by the way for Christmas

oh I see well it would have been nice to have had him with us liven things up a bit lovely boy do give him my love when you see him next Well dear it's been lovely hearing from you and I'll get a nice turkey I've got a lot of booze in   yes I know dear still he drinks beer doesn't he most men drink beer   well be seeing you darling lovely to hear   yes yes goodbye oh what time train will you be getting   I see well I'll wait until I hear from you on the phone   yes yes goodbye darling take care of yourself and my love to

'Good morning and how are we today?'

'Bloody rotten if you must know.'

'Why is that – tell me more?'

Silence. Patient confronted psychiatrist. Woman and man. She looked at the thin hair he had carefully placed over his yellow husk. Thin lips, almost no lips. Thick hands, bunches of spiders on his knuckles. He wrote or doodled, leaning forward, back.

'I don't like your madness.'

'What do you mean by that Sandra?'

Pen poised, ready to stab yet another record. She could not see his eyes, the light bounced, spiralled in his spectacles. Black tentacles crept from his nostrils. In the distance a woman screamed.

'Won't you explain further Sandra – tell me what you are thinking?'

She did not hear him, did not choose to, she waited with the walls for the screams to subside. She saw the hospital staff in their hygienic armour of white approach a struggling body. The raising of a needle, the filling of it, hands holding the body down, eyes unable to see when the needle would sink into the flesh. Soon the whimpering would fill in the cracks, bury itself in some closet room, behind a locked door.

She knew he would continue writing even if she did not say anything. Every gesture noted. She looked towards the window. Out there another world; were they still there waiting? No, they had gone, and meanwhile she had to cope with this clown. Those tentacles crept out of his ears. She stared at a stain on his waistcoat, like semen between the wrinkles, above the separation over his paunch.

'I really don't like you and I have nothing more to say.'

He smiled, showing a hole where a lizard struggled between rocks. In a space between clouds some gigantic bird wheeled, then plummeted down. White on white the snow against walls. As white as God's beard. She closed her eyes. Prismatic colours rose and fell.

'Tell me about the journey you took – why did you…?'

'No.'

Wind ruffled snow. The north wind bringing the sound of ice. She saw again three gulls circle the ship's mast, and heard the movement of wood against ice; saw the ice bergs like fallen statues move slowly past. Points of light from islands pinpricked the disturbed darkness. Gull cries echoed the endless cries of the dead from the ocean depths. How many of the dead had she awoken from their full-fathomed dreams? Bless you all, she muttered.

'What was that?'

'Fuck you.'

He laughed, a gasping kind of sound escaped through the hole.

'That's your reaction in analysis to me, don't be influenced, don't be moved, don't be lured into reacting to me.'

'It's not how you live that matters it's how you die that's important.' She said, watching him scratch the paper, a nicotine-stained finger curled round the pen, or tapped it with mechanical precision. He pulled back his sleeve and scratched his hairy wrist. She knew he was really looking at his watch.

'Well I think that's it for today Sandra.' He took his spectacles off; perhaps his eyes went with them? She could see nothing there that might even resemble eyes.

She escaped into the corridor, where Thomas waylaid her. At least he had eyes, washed-out blue, focusing always on some point to the left of her head.

'You believe me don't you, even if no one else does, you do don't you?' he said, catching hold of her arm, 'you believe that I'm Judas Iscariot reincarnated, you see I have positive proof, the evidence is all in my book, at least it will be when I've written it, and God is Mrs. Carr, and my friend Bob is Jesus Christ.'

'What are you going to call your book Thomas?'

'God's Joke.'

They walked into the ward, where she joined the queue for her medicine.

'Blessings on you from the Holy Mother of God herself oh Jesus Christ have mercy on your sins you cunt you bloody fucking cunt.' Said Mrs. Carr, undoing her nightdress.

'Now Annie you know you mustn't do that – be a good girl do yourself up.' A nurse said, placing her hand on the woman's shoulder. Somewhere above a man groaned; somewhere else a woman laughed. Nearby a high-pitched voice cried 'Where's mummy where's my mummy I want my mummy.'

'May the blessed Virgin shit on you – shit shit shit.' Shouted Annie Carr, frantic fingers plucked at her nightie.

Sandra awaited her turn for the pills she would later spit out in the lavatory. A new patient entered the ward, screaming between two orderlies.

'I don't want to come here – what are you doing to me – I'm going home right now – leave me – let me go you can't keep me here you have no right – no right whatsoever – I want to go home.' The patient's voice trailed off, rose again as white coated robots surrounded her. The needle produced, raised. The screams into inevitable whimpers, as one more person was subdued into drugged submissiveness; would later wake up, dazed, glaze-eyed, nod into helplessness before the authority of 'feel better – that's right – no need to worry you're in good hands now – we're here to help you.'

'I had a dream about you last night Sandra,' Thomas whispered, 'where your head had been cut off, it was delivered to me all bandaged up with blood dripping through – perhaps you are John the Baptist – yes that must be it.'

'But Thomas last week I was the Virgin Mary.' He did not reply, and wandered off down the corridors of his Jerusalem.

Sandra bent over the lavatory and watched the pills fall, she flushed them away.

'Sandra – Sandra are you there – your mother is on the 'phone do you want to speak to her?'

'No.'

'She sends her love.'

The Red Queen breathing through the tunnel. Her face at the bottom of the lavatory, grinned up. Flush her away. Sandra sat for some time in the lavatory, the only place she could be by herself and not be distracted, and go back over the journey; even so their voices interrupted 'It's all in the head you must realise that – in the head in the head inthehead inthehead inthehead…' and she saw the doctor's faceless presence behind his desk, like the painting 'Le Principe du Plaisir', by Magritte, except the figure in the painting was infinitely better, more pleasing. Then there was the Red Queen's face, one eye open; even when dead her mother, no doubt, would be watching her. And Clive – what of Clive? Frightened of his own madness; seeing her actions, reactions as an interpretation of what he considered a madness just round the corner for himself. Young, younger than herself, blond and beautiful with a little old man tucked away somewhere, who popped out unexpected and snarled at her, or worse: turned away, back into his next masterpiece. Then all the spectres who possessed him throughout the night, all with different ways of snoring, various positions in sleep. She had grown to love them all, admittedly she feared a few, especially the little boy part of him that stood apart, helpless, frightened, while they in white coats pinned her down. He had never forgiven her for that, for losing control, and unable to forgive himself for allowing it to happen.

'Sandra lunch is ready – Sandra are you all right – what are you doing so long in there?'

'What do you think I'm doing – I'm flushing my dreams away.'

'Well hurry up dear lunch is being served.'

'I would prefer not to have caviar today Nurse just a little of the duck with orange thank you.'

She opened the door, the nurse looked suspiciously in.

'If you want to see the remains of my dreams why don't you look in there?' Sandra moved aside. The nurse clicked her teeth, and took mental note of the patient's words.

'You can add to your brief that the patient did not resist to having her dreams looked at.'

The nurse pushed the patient out, back into the ward, where the sound of knives scraped the edge of plates. Some knives remained as motionless as the person confronting the food.

'May the Holy Mother of God bless you and be food for what we praise in God the fucking father and Satan in the Holy Ghost lamb brought to slaughter.' Annie Carr shouted, pushing out her left breast, dipping it in the gravy.

'Naughty Annie, now you know we told you that if you don't behave yourself you will have to have your meals by yourself.'

'Oh forgive me for what I have not done – on your bended knees and may God strike me dead if I tell lies.' Annie Carr slid under the table, tore off her nightdress, and on all fours gave herself to the linoleum. Two orderlies rushed in. They struggled with the heaving mass of flesh. The other patients carried on eating, chatting to themselves, or each other. Sandra looked across at the young boy who had only arrived yesterday, who had not spoken a word, had not eaten anything. He stared back, through her; what dream screen did he see? Curly dark hair showed through his pyjama top. As if he knew she wanted to place her head there, her fingers in the warm moist nest, he placed his hand on the hairs, and smiled.

'You must be ready for the invasion they are disguised as dwarfs and walk about in the parks, I've got my hammer ready for them, so at least I shall be all right, and I'm making a special bomb to destroy them.' Said an old man at the end of the table. No one took any notice, they had heard his warnings day in, day out. The bomb he kept under the bed, at least that's where it had been until they took it away. A contraption that had been improvised out of lead piping, ball-bearings and wire.

Someone started crying. Another person laughed. Sandra left the table and went into the dormitory. She lay on her bed and stared at the ceiling.

'You can't lie down now dear, it's time for your occupational therapy – painting isn't it for you this afternoon?'

'I don't want to.'

'Well you can't go to sleep now Sandra.'

She felt under the mattress, yes the journal was still there, she took it out and began writing.

'Sandra please get up now and go across for your painting session.'

'Sandra it's time to get up. Sandra your meal is ready. It's time to go to bed. Sandra take your pills. It's time for your treatment. Sandra get your potty. You're late. Sandra do your homework. Pick that up. Are you in there Sandra? Don't do that. Stop snivelling and whining like a child. Sandra do her peepees now. Sandra do her two-twos now. Sandra don't wear your best dress. Put on that coat Sandra. Put that book down when I'm talking to you. Don't go around like that in your bare feet you'll get athlete's foot. Don't go in for petting with men Sandra it leads to other things. Sandra do you hear me…?'

Yes I hear you all my mothers and fathers will you never stop? Stop.

She made her way to Block C, but did not enter. Instead she walked the grounds and made paintings with her footprints in the snow. A solitary bird, a hooded midget nun, on a bare branch looked down and seemed to wink. Once she had understood the language of birds, now no longer, it took all her time to understand her own language, and that of those who attempted communication. Once there had been the subterranean language with the underground forces. If speech at all then it was the spaces between words, and the echoes the words left, or what might be really meant under the surface. She knew, had known. No longer knew. Only remembered. In the recollection, pictures, words, visions, thoughts, images built themselves into citadels, gigantic towers that toppled with the weight of it all; the top heavier than the foundations. Last events came first, the beginning at the end, or suddenly reversed, or slid into panels mid-way. Had ECT done that – damn them? She shuddered, as though the wires were attached to her head there under the branches. Branches shaped in a design by the wind. They shape one into a walky talky doll with all the correct responses. Squeeze me here and I squeak. She squeaked, and watched the nun fly off. Snow sea-sprayed on to her face.

The boy, who never spoke, approached. He held out a box of chocolates. She thanked him. He smiled, inclined his head, like a dog, waiting for her to throw a stick. Then she saw what he was really applying himself to; he had his own stick to play with. She walked away quickly, nausea rising. The Exit gates were wide open. If she ran past the porters' lodge perhaps… but the sound of traffic defeated her; sound of heavy Red Army boots would be out there, they would be waiting for her. She threw the chocolates into an area of untrampled snow.

She sat in the rose arbour and opened her journal.

Today I do not know the date

There is snow, heavy on the surrounding hedges. I can no longer remember how long I have been here and yet I count the days for when I am discharged. They say 'soon'. 'You are making progress.' It is all pretence, on their part, as well as mine.

DIALOGUE WITH ANALYST

A1:   Come in (long pause). How are you today?

P1:   I had this dream last night.

A2:   Yes?

P2:   I was playing the piano and suddenly the keys went soft, I noticed they were my fingers, that in fact my fingers had changed into keys. I looked over the keyboard, inside the piano was my father wrapped in cellophane. He was dead, at least I thought he was until I bent over and peered closer, he rose and his hand broke through the cellophane, tried to grab me and pull me down.

A3:   Ummhuh.

P3:   And, ahh, I thought I'd bring that up. (Pause) Bring the, ahh, dream up I mean, not him, my father.

A4:   Ahh, it makes sense.

P4:   Then I had this fantasy (pause) that is, ahh (pause) after ahh I woke up.

A5:   Yes.

P5:   I would find my father and stab him in the back, which of course means I really want him to fuck me (pause) ahh and then I was angry because of the guilt.

A6:   The logical sequence.

P6:   The logical sequence, fits into the pattern (pause) doesn't it?

A7:   More or less – yes.

P7:   Against myself primarily, but (pause) ahh well I've planned it all out I know where he works for some death-aid place (pause) sorry I mean ahh deaf-aid – it's along Miller Street, and you know how crowded it can be there.

A8:   Yes it can get very crowded.

P8:   Well, ahh, I would (pause) wait for him to come out of his office at 5.30 – his office isn't actually on Miller Street but in Bond Street (pause) do you know it?

A9:   Yes, I know the street.

P9:   Well there's a little question there, ahh, the decision of this as a possibility is becoming more crystallized.

A10:   Ummhuh.

P10:   So this fantasy has triggered all sorts of other things off (pause) for instance, ahh, if I project my father image on to someone else.

A11:   Ummhuh.

P11:   But that's another dimension.

A12:   The other side of yourself.

P12:   Not myself at all (pause) I see the whole situation as an outsider looking on. I have not felt myself as

A13: Ummhuh (pause). So there's kind of, it's sort of the existentialist approach.

P13: I have to sort of, what, struggle around to try and find something that describes it all and the terminology used, I make no guarantee of its accuracy.

A14: OK now Wednesday at four?

P14: Wednesday at four.

A15: Goodbye.

P15: Goodbye.

Patient and Analyst satisfied. But myself? Only impatience at his stupidity in listening and believing in the radio he switches on.

Sandra closed the journal. Opening her mouth she waited for the snow to fall in. She heard footsteps of someone approaching. The old man shuffled by, furtively looking over his shoulder.

'Ah did you see him – one of them actually here disguised as a dwarf, I must get my bomb?'

He wandered off. In the distance she saw flames, which she went towards. A rubbish heap being burnt. She could smell the burning of flesh. Perhaps they cremated those who were never discharged? Something scurried into the bushes – a rat. She felt hungry, remembered the chocolates, and went across the lawns to where she had thrown them. Like a thief she quickly put them in her pocket. In a lavatory she crammed them two by two into her mouth.

Disinfectant, steel trolleys, closed doors, shouts, murmurs, screams. Scurry of porters, orderlies, nurses. Patients in dressing-gowns stared out of windows, or were fascinated by something on a wall, in the stone floor. Smells of urine, cabbage and rubber. So many wards, all looking the same; corridors upon corridors. She wandered along an endless one, dark, empty. A door opened. She was pulled into a pitch-dark room. She recognised the boy's smell – the smell of water dead flowers leave, as he pressed her against his body. She pushed him and heard him cry out. She fled.

In Block C she joined the half dozen patients who were in the middle of describing their paintings.

'This is me in the middle.'

'But it looks like a horse.'

'It's me and above are two moons in eclipse.'

'That looks more like you.'

'Hallo Sandra where's your painting – the one you did last week?'

'I destroyed it – I've done another though it's outside.'

'Well fetch it and we'll have a look.'

'I can't – anyway the wind has probably wiped it out.'

'Very well, if you feel like doing one now Sandra you have time.'

She thought of Clive's paintings; the need for posterity. How much better to create like the Navajo Indians, beginning at sunrise in the desert, a sand painting that would be rubbed out by sundown. A desert landscape with wild horses galloping across. Sand rippled. Landscape only disturbed by the wind. In a grain of sand the whole universe – something like that, Blake put. He had visions. A God who laughed, belched, snored and picked His nose. Her God had been straight out of Blake, long snowy beard and snowy locks, and in His face every conceivable landscape.

'That's a funny face Sandra.'

'It's God.'

'Looks like a lump of shit to me.' A patient said, making up her face with paint brushes. Someone else suddenly woke up and cried out 'The light, the black one, ahh, that stabs in the dark, ahh, because, ahh, I haven't, what, looked at them from the outside, of what this is a step towards, in that if I don't make these reasons.'

'Now Charles what have you done to-day?'

'I've switched off the connecting line to the President.'

'Yes well – but I mean you haven't done any work have you Charles, you've been asleep the whole afternoon?'

'The connection has been switched off.' He collapsed over the table and went back to sleep.

It was time for tea. They filed out, back to their wards. Back to the trolley where the wolves pounced on pieces of cake and biscuits.

'There's a visitor to see you Sandra.'

She looked up and saw Clive stride in.

'Hallo how are you?'

'Fine – and you?'

'Fine.'

Silence. He sat down on the edge of the chair. On the edge of the bed she spread out her legs as he bent over her.

'Cold today isn't it?'

'Yes colder than yesterday.'

'Yes – temperature has fallen.'

'Yes.'

'Cigarette?'

'Thanks.'

Silence. He pulled her off the bed, carried her towards the mirror.

'Still you're nice and warm in here – best place to be really.'

'Yes.'

Silence. Body to body. Body part of body. One body. The spaces between limbs.

'The food OK?'

'Oh it's all right.'

Silence. She took him in her mouth. He moved with the rhythm of her tongue.

'Oh I forgot – something for you – just a little something – here.' She took the box of chocolates from him, and smiled, looking at his hand. Fine boned, veins showing through like a Chinese water colour. What other skin had that hand explored?

'Been working well?'

'On and off – you know.'

'And the teaching?'

'Just the same – same old rut.'

'How are your parents?'

'Fine – sent their love to you.'

'Well I…'

'Do you still…?'

'Sorry you were saying?'

'Ought to be going.'

'Yes.'

'Well goodbye – take care – see you again soon.'

'Goodbye.'

'Goodbye.' He bent over and pecked her on the cheek.

'Don't eat them all at once.' He said, indicating the chocolates, and strode out.

'Time for group session.' A nurse shouted. Shuffle of feet, chairs put in a circle. Patients from other wards came in. Three doctors surveyed the scene. Annie Carr tripped in and made the sign of the cross over each person.

'Sit down Annie – now who would like to begin?'

'I would like to say that I think the food here is pig's muck.' Said an enormous woman.

'It's better than what you'd get in the nick I can tell you.' Said another woman.

'I think there ought to be two televisions it's not fair just having the one and Mrs. Whatshername hogs it all the time I never see what I want to see.'

'I want to know when I can leave?'

'I don't think it's fair being woken up at six in the morning.'

'Someone has stolen my slippers.'

'I have a poem here I'd like to read it's called "The Trees Aching Green" – when the trees move…'

'We don't want to hear any of your crappy poems.'

'When the trees begin to walk…'

'I want to know when I can go home?'

'Naked I stand in the roots…'

'Imagine him naked ahhha.' All the patients laughed. The doctors remained silent, yawned, or doodled, or looked at the clock.

'An earwig crawled into my ear Doctor and it's eating away my insides – I wish to have an X-ray please.'

'Looks as though it's eating away the outside as well.'

'The roots of my heaven leave holes in the sky…'

'You've got holes in your socks if that's what you mean?'

'Can we please have our eggs soft boiled?'

'I want to know when I can be discharged?'

'Two televisions instead of one.'

'The branches of my hell leave traces in the mirror…'

'Not surprised the way you look.'

'Someone's stolen my pearls.'

'Can we have two eggs instead of one for breakfast?'

'I want to go home.' Someone shouted, rose, and made for the corridor. A nurse brought him back.

'Has anyone anything else to say?' A doctor asked. Silence, apart from coughs, clicking of knitting needles, and someone snoring.

'Well I think that's it for this afternoon – thank you.' The doctor said, smiling round the circle. He and the other doctors marched out, followed by a few patients, whom they ignored. Cries of 'When can I...?' 'Please tell me Doctor when…' 'I demand an X-ray so you'll believe me you'll see the earwig for yourself…' Cries that bounced back onto the patients, leaving them with each other, from whom they turned away, turned into themselves, or the walls, the floors, the windows that looked on to concrete blocks.

Sandra went into the dormitory and lay down. Someone opposite muttered in her sleep. Someone else bent over paper bags. In the distance a man shouted 'No don't do it I don't – don't want it – leave me alone.' Two nurses entered with the Charge Nurse, they marched down the line of beds.

'What's this Sandra aren't we feeling well?'

'I'm tired.'

'You can't sleep here now you know.' She went back into the ward and sat in a corner near the window. An old woman in a wheelchair stared at her, without blinking. Oh God, she's dead, Sandra thought, and turned away. Somewhere beyond the buildings Clive would be striding towards a yellow circle enclosed in a green triangle. Or perhaps a yellow triangle between white circles, a triangle he would enter.

A dry rasping cough startled her. She turned round and the old woman bent over. Sandra moved away and went into the area for television. The boy was there, staring at his fingers, motionless on his knees. She walked up the corridor, back again.

'Sandra come and sort out some counters.' A nurse called out.

'No.' She went and looked for Thomas, he was busy writing.

'Hi.' She bent over and tried to see what he had written, minute words crawled into each other across the paper.

'Is that God's Joke you're writing?'

'Just some notes – I think I've reached the point where I realise that I am betraying myself.'

'I should think by now Christ has forgiven you Thomas.'

'How can I know that He – Bob – I mean He can't speak and whenever I try and speak to Him He has such an accusing look in his nose.'

'How do you mean I mean eh how can you see that in his nose?'

'It points straight out at me.' He continued writing.

'I've seen God's face Thomas did you know that?'

He did not answer, but went on writing. She moved away, and went back to the ward. A young girl was silently crying. The old woman had gone back to her death-like mask. A group of women sorted out the coloured counters, putting them in polythene bags. A woman was trying on a wig.

'What you want that for – it's exactly the same as your own hair?' Someone asked.

'Well I got this lobotomy op coming up and they shave the head you see – nice isn't it – they designed it specially so it would look like my own hair?'

Sandra opened her journal at random.

I don't remember that day as a day – not surprising – for a long time no day seemed like a day, no night seemed like a night. But that particular day has no shape in my memory. I used to mark the time by meals, but as I believe we are given several sets of meals in each real day – about half a dozen sets of breakfast, lunch, tea and dinner in each twelve hours – this was not much help.

She turned several pages and continued reading:

CONVERSATION WITH TWO DOCTORS

Dr. X: Sandra, I wish to ask you something. I'm holding a pen here. Do you see this pen?

S.: No.

Dr. X: Dr. Y, do you see this pen?

Dr. Y: Yes, I see the pen.

Dr. X: Sandra, how is it when I show you the pen, you say, no you don't see it, and Dr. Y says yes, he does see it. How is it he says yes and you say no?

S.: Well… ah the doctor says he doesn't see it?

Dr. Y: I do see it.

S.: You do see it?

Dr. X: What do you say, Sandra?

S.: I do see the pen.

Dr. X: You do see the pen?

S.: Unnhhh.

Dr. X: No, wait, you tell me. I've got the pen here. Do you
see the pen?
S.: No, I don't see it.

I see an endless road, white-glittering under the sun's rays,
glittering like a needle; above the remorseless sun weighing down the trees and houses under its electric rays. How
can I explain, describe that to them? They would never
understand. How ridiculous he looked holding that pen,
nodding, grinning up at the other doctor. What a relief
to get away from them and hear a newly arrived patient
exclaim, 'I am St. Michael the Archangel and the Red
Horse of the Apocalypse. You might say I have delusions of
grandeur, but like Christ, I glorify myself for my Father's
sake. For additional proof, I refer you to metaphysicians
and Jehovah's Witnesses. I am in disguise and one might
say a blessing in disguise.'

Sandra turned the pages over and began writing.

Have just seen C., and saw myself seeing him, saw him
seeing me, or rather not seeing me. His visits now have
become a duty; as soon as he's here he wants to leave,
obviously can't stand the role of visitor with sick person.
I shall write and tell him not to come here anymore. No
point. Nothing. If I love him still it is only love in memory.

Sandra paused, looked out of the window, some gulls
circled above the grey buildings, tips of their wings
caught in the fading light. She thought she heard the
sound of waves breaking, the rush and sliding of pebbles, but it was only the rush-hour traffic. Out there was

a world that carried on its daily duties, and somewhere they might be waiting for her, waiting for her to help in the Cause. But what Cause? She had almost forgotten what it was all about, what it was they wanted of her; like a dream now, the electric waves that had sent messages through her body had disappeared, the Cosmic Forces gone – gone. But not her memory, they hadn't obliterated that with their injections, pills and tentacles on her head. She looked across at the woman with her wig, she held it up for other women to admire. What would she be like after they had operated on her brain? And all because she was a compulsive house cleaner.

She suddenly felt claustrophobic, the smell of women penetrated her nose, mouth, ears and eyes. She went again into the dormitory, where it was dark, silent. She lay down and slid into black velvet. A sea of velvet that tossed her gently, and somewhere above her the sound of ice breaking. If I go back to the beginning of it all... but there is no beginning, and in the description I lose the threads. How many days, nights she had attempted going back over the journey, always it appeared in flashes, like a film running backwards, at top speed, a few pictures were stills, frozen, hovered there while others piled up. A landscape with snow, and the north wind god telling her to move in another direction. A ship's mast in a park, no, wrong again, a heavy cross leaned towards the west, and there was the mast, a ship sliding into dock, moving slowly below the town, in air it seemed. A hotel room overlooking rail tracks, the shuttle of trains, wagons throughout the night. Before then, before I arrived there, how did it begin? Let me see…

Someone groaned across the way. Sandra opened her eyes and peered into the darkness, a huddled shape moved, jerked towards her. She sat up. The smell of stale bread and beef breathed over her.

'Go away.' She shouted at the old woman. 'Go away do you hear?' The old woman laughed and crouched over the bed. 'Nurse she's at it again.' Sandra screamed and sprang off the bed, and ran out.

'Listen that old hag has got out of bed really she can walk she's there go in now honestly if you don't believe me go in now…' The nurse shook her head, clicked her teeth, and marched into the dormitory. Sandra behind her. The old woman lay snoring in her own bed.

'Well she's just got back – honestly she was up a minute ago.'

'Poor old thing she's asleep as usual Sandra you must have been dreaming.'

'I wasn't.'

'She hasn't got out of that bed for eighteen months she's quite incapable of walking Sandra so don't be so silly.'

Ugh, the monster, a clever monster at that, Sandra thought, and went back to her bed.

'You can't sleep now Sandra – you know you're not supposed to be in here at this time of day so come along now.'

She went and watched the television. A newsreel shot of bombs being dropped in an area the pilot had marked out for him on a map. Someone started laughing.

'Shutup.' Someone else said, and concentrated on the picture that had changed to a girl rising in slow motion out of a sparkling sea, following an animated bambi.

'The doctor is human you know yes he's human I know now he's human 'cos he farted today when I saw him.' Someone said, and collapsed into silence.

'Yes she left it all to charity it's a mortal sin that shouldn't be allowed but these old people get cranky don't they funny how they go all queer when they get past a certain age.'

'Such a shock for her…'

'A loud fart it was and the smell was strong.'

'Shutup.'

'And I told Jack to see a lawyer not right leaving it all to a dog's home is it?'

'Have you seen Beryl's wig it looks just like her real hair – less trouble it will be really?'

'So Jack's going to see a lawyer and get it sorted out.'

'I mean when you hear a fart and smell a fart then you know a man's a man and he's human.'

'Will you shutup.'

'Just like her own hair, same colour and everything, cost a bomb I'm sure – had it specially designed for her – can't tell the difference at all.'

Someone changed the television channel. Screams of protest.

'Well you weren't watching anyway just natter natter natter.'

'That's not fair we were watching.'

'No you fucking wasn't.'

'No need for that.'

Silence. A picture came on of a table laden with food.

'Looks nice doesn't it?'

'Not poisoned like it is here.'

They leaned forward and watched the picture intently. They leaned back and swallowed their saliva; carried on chattering, nose-picking, knitting; fingers plucked at buttons, cigarettes, fingers at fingers, a battle of insects.

Sandra moved heavily away, and looked at the clock. An hour to go before supper. She saw Thomas staring into oblivion.

'What you thinking – you look miles away?'

He did not answer, nor look at her. Obviously in one of his moods. She persevered.

'Thomas tell me about God's Joke?' But he persevered in his silence. She put her hand out as if to touch him, but there was that feeling again – overpowering from his body – his grey mottled skin would not feel like skin to touch, but some horrible substance that would congeal under her hands. She looked round the ward. People slept, or muttered to themselves, to each other, or were transfixed by some part of their anatomy; a lot seemed concerned with their hands, as though they were palm reading. Some nurses laughed behind a closed door. She looked again at the clock. Soon it would be supper, soon it will be over, and the long night crawled ahead of her.

She went into the dormitory once more, hastily looked over for the lump of senility – the old woman was not there. Sandra looked quickly round and saw a shadow move or rather lurch from the other shadows, and the old woman, cackling, stumbled towards her. Sandra quickly went over to her own bed, brought out her journal and ran out.

She found an uninhabited space where she pulled up a chair and table, but someone entered her new-found territory. It was Thomas, blinking like a bat behind his spectacles.

'Wondered if you'd care to read this and let me know what you think about it?' He handed her a wad of paper covered in his spider writing.

'Is this God's Joke?' She asked, looking at the pages, moving her hand quickly away from his that still held on to the paper.

'Yes – just rough though – notes really.'

'But I can't read it – your writing is absolutely illegible Thomas.'

'What if I read some of it to you?'

'If you like.'

He pulled up a chair, cleared his throat, cleared it in such a way she half expected to see a frog jump out, or some of the grey inner substance.

'In the beginning when all was space, space not as we know it, but an infinite space, with nothing, no light, no darkness, God had a dream. The dream was a desert with horizon, and then He woke up, and felt very lonely, very bored and…'

'What a load of old bullshit.' Someone passing by, shouted. Thomas paused, bit his lip, frowned.

'Where was I – oh yes – bored and He thought if He could dream such dreams why couldn't He create the dream into reality. So He… are you listening?'

'Yes, yes go on very interesting.'

'He created the desert and the sky, and again he felt lonely, and very bored, so he went to sleep again, and had another dream… oh damn it's supper time – I'll read some more after OK?'

Sandra nodded, and followed him to the dining hall, where she joined the queue and awaited her turn. She ate quickly, amidst the usual babble, scraping of plates, coughing and spluttering.

'I'll see you back in my ward Thomas OK?'

She went outside, and stood on the entrance steps. In the distance a dog howled. The snow made points of whiteness in the dark, and the stars reflected their points, but no longer did they charge her pulse; the transmission had been cut off. There was no moon. She no longer moved with the weather, no longer a creature of the night. The wind changed its direction of its own accord. The dog's howl entered her. Whining, she ran into the grounds, across frozen lumps of earth towards the North Star that hung suspended beyond the gates.

The gates were shut. She moved along by the railings, in deep snow, shivering, and looked at the row of identical houses the other side. She stood for some time looking in at a window where the curtains had not been drawn. A woman watched television. A man on a bed, read a newspaper. A naked light bulb burned between them. The woman turned round, got up, and drew the curtains. Sandra moved back slowly to the entrance steps, and sat down on the top step, breathing over her hands. No signs. No messages. Where had they gone? Supposing if they – the doctors – everyone were right, it had all been in her head?

She peered through her fingers at the white and black landscape, and watched the snow fall. Already her tracks had been covered, but those made by cars on the winding road remained, thin rust-coloured patterns. She rose and went inside, up to the ward, or rather into a parrot house.

Those who were not chattering, stalked the room, or fluttered on chairs, made stabbing movements with knitting needles, reams of coloured wool spilled on to the floor, dribbled yellow and red between flapping arms. Someone croaked, another barked. A mouth opened, closed, opened again, no sound came. But eventually a howl did emerge. Doors opened, and in rushed the keepers. The howl continued. People turned their heads, froze in contorted positions, as the keepers bent over a young girl struggling on the floor; her head curiously twisted; the white of her eyes showed through dark feathers, damp with sweat. The howl changed into a gurgle, the gurgle to gasps, as the body writhed in the net of arms. And like a huge octopus the group moved slowly out of the room. The girl's shoe remained, on its side. Someone kicked it across the floor. The knitting needles pierced the air, click click click, and bodies took up their preceding positions, and went through the motions of survival of the fittest.

Sandra went into a lavatory and sat down. She watched her legs shake, her hands came up as if warding off blows. She heard someone come in, being sick, coughing followed, then muttering.

'Damn them – fuck 'em bastards – more earwigs, not just one – nurse – nurse come here and see thousands of 'em, it must have been that shepherd's pie – they must have come from that – nurse come and see.'

Sandra looked at her knees, as if they belonged to someone else, they nudged, knocked against each other, in some strange communication of their own.

'Come along dear – it's all right – there now feel better?' A nurse said.

'Look at 'em wriggling away down there – that's evidence for you.'

'Now don't be silly dear come watch television we like watching tele don't we now – come along.'

187

'That thing is plugged in you know and watches me they think I don't know about the earwigs they are planting.'

'Yes yes come along now there's a good girl.' The good girl shuffled out.

Sandra stood on the lavatory seat and opened the tiny window, where she looked out on a narrow space of darkness. The window sill had a hard crust of snow impregnated with pigeon tracks, a part ruffled in the middle, where the bird's feathers must have brushed against the snow. She looked up and saw the edge of the moon, like a broken off finger nail. A train rattled by and left an echo between the buildings. Someone next door breathed heavily, loud farts filled the air. Sandra closed the window and jumped down. She went out and washed her hands. A woman was sticking false eye-lashes on, swearing under her breath.

'Don't know why I bother she never looks at me now.' The woman said, twisting her mouth, smiling at herself.

'You don't have to bother do you dear you're still young you don't have to bother with makeup – lovely hair you have is that its real colour?' The woman looked at Sandra in the mirror, moved over to her, and still looking in the mirror, she stroked Sandra's hair.

'Lovely and soft – you're lovely and soft – what's the matter – oh well be like that.'

Sandra moved away, followed by the woman shouting, swearing. Through the swing door, in a backward glance, Sandra saw a crumpled face, an eyelash quivered on a rouged cheek.

Music greeted her in the ward. A party jerked people into action, or non-action. A table laden with jellies, small grey sandwiches and jugs of orange juice. Women danced with women, the men smoked and watched, or slyly went off to their secret horde of hard liquor. Thomas came up, bowed and asked if she cared to dance. She shrank away.

'I couldn't find you after supper – wanted to read you the rest – ahh I…'

'Perhaps tomorrow Thomas?'

The girl who had earlier thrown a fit was brought in, stiff, glaze-eyed, she sat down and contemplated her finger nails. People moved away from the girl. They knew who to avoid, not to avoid, so that little groups formed round the room, watched over by a few charge nurses on the fringe. Two or three men swayed in, burping, spluttering with laughter.

'Enjoying ourselves are we then – that's right?' Before Sandra could answer the nurse moved along, nodding, smiling at everyone.

In the alcove Sandra noticed the boy, who had given her the chocolates, he stared at the television, which was not turned on. She walked into the dormitory, and sat on her bed, eyes closed. Laughter and music from the ward entered, drifted away, entered again. Two women came in, whispering. Sandra pretended to be asleep, and watched them through half closed eyes. They gently embraced at first, but soon they clawed each other, like animals in a fight. Sandra shut her eyes tightly, but she heard the two women panting, swearing, and soon the bed creaked. She felt the sweat run between her breasts. She opened her eyes, shut them; did not want to look, but looked. She held her breath, as the women's breathing came heavy and fast. Arms and legs flew everywhere, or mingled. One of the women crouched in a praying position between huge thighs, mottled skin marked with bruises and thick purple veins.

Sandra got up and moved quietly down between the beds. One of the women shrieked with laughter.

'Getting bored darling – come and join us?'

Out of the corner of her eyes, she saw a puffy red face, a pink and yellow tongue curled about itself, protruding.

Back in the ward someone offered her a piece of jelly. She refused, and sat down. The atmosphere was hot and smoky. A group in the middle attempted Knees Up Mother Brown. Another group sang old songs. Annie Carr sat on the floor, between her spread legs a long orange strip of wool dangled; she was conducting with the knitting needles, and singing a hymn in a strange cracked voice 'All Things Bright and Beautiful'. Sandra turned towards the girl and asked her name, there was no response, apart from a slight twitching of the girl's hands. Thomas came over, and sighing, sat down next to Sandra.

'How can you say Annie Carr is God, Thomas – I mean look at her now – just look at her?'

'We all have our disguises.' He replied, taking his spectacles off, and wiping them with a grubby handkerchief. The needle in the record stuck in a groove and the words 'All I need is love' blared out over and over again. Someone stopped it, people hardly seemed to notice, but went on kicking into the air, swaying, bumping against each other.

'I have this buzzing in my head – strange it doesn't seem to go – had it for days now.' Thomas said, shaking his head from side to side. 'As if a fly has got in or something.'

The strains of a last waltz came over, and everyone drifted apart, and looked at the remains of food, crumbs on the table, the floor. A few couples moved slowly round, with eyes closed, trying to kiss, avoiding kisses. One old man collapsed, smiling happily. Another man helped him up, holding a whisky bottle to his mouth. The old man gurgled, then sucked on the bottle. Sandra edged her way into the dormitory. The women were no longer there. She undressed and got into bed. The others came in, giggling.

Soon there was just the sound of the clock, and breathing, wheezing, dream murmurs and bodies turning over.

The long night stretched out. Wind rattled the windows, and snow mixed with hail pounded like small fists against glass. In the middle of the dormitory, a nurse read or slept under a lamp. Sandra stared at this light until it spun from its orbit and approached. Right at the very beginning – but there was no beginning. Vague notes for the basis of a shape. The first section interrupted by the last. No continuous movement. A starting point somewhere. Chord superimposed on chords. The pendulum swung back.

I am a bird hovering, searching for human shape, from the vapours of air, space, I settle into the waters of the womb and dream ancestral dreams. I am the Lady of the Lake, my hand rises out of a circle of light. Merlin's spectre emerges from a crack in the wall. I climb up enamel cliffs and step into the shape of a woman I no longer know, or is it I know her only too well? And having been outside her I see this woman go through the motions of preparing herself for her lover. For it will soon be time for his arrival; appropriate music is being sent over the radio. Soon the familiar turn of the key, followed by his voice. She is startled by the sound of her own voice, words that have wavelengths stretching beyond the walls, reaching out to the dead. They are there listening. A few are jealous. Others protective. Their faces line the ceiling; cling to trees; file slowly by in white ships. In the gardens there are messages in the placing of twigs and leaves. A blackbird gives a note of warning. I am prepared for the 'phone, for this woman's mother.

'Hallo darling how are you?'

'Hallo hallo hallo how are you how are you hallo darling hallo darling.'

'Hallo hallo are you there – darling what's the matter?'

'What's the matter what's the matter what's the matter?'

Silence, followed by heavy breathing. Then click, and just the hum, the breathing of those listening in. Let her think I'm mad, let them all think that, so readily they will claim their superiority over fear.

Three lights from the houses opposite. The danger is over. Clive stands in the doorway, smiling, questioning. What did she do with herself all day, was she better? Three years she had lived with this man and loved him. For millions of years she had loved him, when they first crawled out of primeval mud together. Yet he still behaved like a guest, claiming no rights, not even to his own existence in this life span. A red light comes on opposite. A warning that he is tired, hungry, a little depressed. He slumps down on the settee, yawns, giving in to his spectre of the moment. I bend over him and attempt to draw out the Knight, with the help of the North Star. But the spectre of his Grandfather refuses the warmth. He is grumpy, petulant, suspicious. The red light still glows from the third window in the top storey across the road. A man sits, bent over, I can see his back, he is taking deep breaths, trying to gain energy for transmitting strength from the stars.

How can I tell Clive my fugitive visions? That I've given my job up, yes I can tell him that, and expect the reaction of: how on earth can we manage? That I've given up smoking, given up eating meat, that I want a child… ah finally it has come to that. But I remain silent and prepare the dinner.

'What's this then?' he laughs, pecks at the vegetables, prodding the carrots, turning them over.

'You're not going in for all that cranky vegetarian stuff are you Sandra?' His grandfather prongs a turnip. Other spectres come and go, fleetingly in a frown, a curl of the lip; an agitated movement of legs, sprawled out after dinner satisfaction.

'Well I don't mind vegetables really – supposed to be good for one.' But listen to what he is really saying, gestures belie what is being said; hand clutches throat. The faces round the walls are in conspiracy.

'I'm worried about you Sandra you have hardly eaten anything, and you say you don't sleep very much lately – what is the matter – shouldn't you see the doctor?' His voice from a great distance. An electric charge vibrates through my left side.

'I'm really living for the first time.' I hear my voice, but the words cannot describe what I feel, what I see, what I hear.

'I honestly don't know love but I think you're not very well – why don't you go and see the doctor tomorrow?' Someone taps on the wall next door; a red light comes on opposite, goes off. The faces watch, listen to a man and woman who act out their parts for each other. I am sliding down bannisters of ivory to a sound I have known from the beginning of time. The woman the man knows tells him she wants a child, that she no longer is taking the pill. The man is astonished, terrified of some future unseen usurper, and makes excuses: the lack of money, the responsibility, temperament, the time is not right, perhaps later when…

Later in bed the man turns away and goes to sleep on the edge of the bed. Hour after hour slide by as I sleep with my eyes open; a lioness guarding her mate, child, prince, king. The spectres come and go, leaping in the darkness, lifting the man's sleeping form into themselves, and stalking the universe until the first faint light brings them tumbling back to snatch the last vestiges of some dream.

The light will gradually build up a ladder of fire against the wall behind the bed. Clive lies in the shadow. The city is still divided outside. The west holds the night, blurred on the horizon. The east shows arrows of light that bring the birds out of their territories.

I walk in the gardens, and know it must have been like this in the beginning. The trees are old, and groan under their own weight and the weight of those who have embedded themselves in the bark. I lean against an oak and feel the grains of wood give strength to my bones. The pulse in my wrist twitches in time with the vibration of the stars. Stars that are gradually disappearing. Looking up at the bedroom window I see the blinds lift with the morning breeze. I have left them all to struggle with Clive, enter his dreams; but soon they will leave, when the sun reaches a certain point, and the ladder against the wall leans into the shadow. Then it will be time for me to return.

Meanwhile I have to go back into the past of this existence; the interpretation lies before me here and now. A rag doll lies on its side. The garden seats have been arranged in a circle. The swing is waiting. I fly through light, space, time. High and higher, beyond the point I desired when a child. A desire and other desires I only now recognise. I descend and enter a garden that seems to be lit from underneath, as if by thousands of glow worms burning in the undergrowth. I move through leaves, fallen branches, as if I am on stilts. My shadow lengthens.

Back in the flat I bend over Clive, he wrestles with his departing dream figures, struggles with the approaching day, smiles, and then remembers. He searches for a cigarette, lights one up, and watches the smoke coil into the particles of dust that form a column in beams of light. Suspicion and accusation disturb the blueness of his eyes; eyes that narrow when looking at the woman who has decided. Words pile up but they are words never uttered. For the woman seems to be in another world, sitting at the end of the bed, staring out of the window. But suddenly he exclaims 'Don't think I don't know – I mean why you want a child now you have reached the age where you think it is about time that soon it will be too late and just because you…' But she turned swiftly upon him and kissed his eyes. He groaned, twisted his head away.

'What are we going to do Sandra?'

He gets dressed, shaves, and leaves, wrestling with the question mark that threatens to destroy a habit; to be a lover was one thing, but a father was something else entirely, and soon the question would turn itself into well we'll see.

I lie on the bed, in the warmth that remains of Clive's body, I can feel a small damp patch under my legs.

Staring at the white wall I see a face appear. White against white. Soon valleys, mountains, forests, rivers, lakes and many oceans appear in the face, in the white hair and long beard. The eyes contain day and night, and in their depths stellar spaces. Each strand of hair is luminous. I know it is God's face. This is the absolute. I am held suspended in a happiness I have never known, nor will ever know again. The face dissolves, and others spring up, those I have appeared with in the past. But this is the last cycle. How ancient I am, all these millions of years travelled through, every spirit of insect, animal and human I have known. Still the journey is not over, and there are those who are determined the destroy me. I have much to learn, and re-learn. The conditioning process of this life now must be discarded. I have been chosen, but cannot choose.

The glow from the garden ascends. The ladder of fire reaches the ceiling. I am walking on air from room to room. The walls breathe and have luminous edges. Those from the other side have melted away. But Death in white sits on the swing, head bent, hooded. Waiting. The chairs in the garden have been re-arranged. The rag doll has been put on one of the seats, a thrush guards her. Is it safe to go out? From the window I can see the street lined both sides with parked cars. Two blue cars parked outside this house, a sign that it is all right. I can't be too careful.

Once outside I can hardly lift one foot in front of the other. The sun burns my energy away. The powers of the moon and the sound of stars only give me strength. I move like a blind person. But the signs are there. As long as I keep within the Controlled Zone I will be safe, outside of that it is enemy territory. The traffic lights are for me all the way. My right side gives me the route to take. But it is all very difficult to learn, to understand. A pain goes through my left side, I have taken the wrong turning. I am out of the Controlled Zone. Two Russian spies are waiting on the corner, just like in a corny film, hiding behind newspapers. The traffic speeds up, then slows down so I can run across the road and into the park.

The spirit is willing but the flesh is weak. I sit down on the damp grass. I cannot go on. But the two spies are approaching rapidly. I have to get up. If they capture me they will use me for their own ends and destroy the Good. Those of the underground movement are nowhere to be seen. Perhaps this is another test – to see if I can manage on my own. It is too much, why aren't they here to help? The password has been relayed from spy to spy, they appear between trees. I move towards the sound of water, where children poke sticks and watch toy sailing boats dip and spin in the pond.

In the distance emerging from the thin greyness of autumn mist a skyscraper that looks like a rocket. The space ship to Mars is only half way on its journey, and every breath I take either speeds it on in space or slows it down. My breath today is short, I am giving them a difficult journey. I suddenly see a friend walking along by the edge of the pond the other side. At least I thought she was a friend, but now I am not too sure. She has haunted me all these millions of years, and like so many of those I meet, she had returned once more only for revenge. The past is catching up, she has seen me and waves. I turn away and see the spies shift behind their newspapers, move from the trees into an open space. The park used to be a shelter from the concrete and steel, it is now another inferno teeming with serpents.

Of course – why hadn't I thought of it before – how stupid? It is this leather coat my mother gave me, I must get rid of it, then I shall be able to move in a free way, be lighter, for her claim weighs heavily upon me, not only the coat, but the watch she also gave me.

I leave the coat and watch in a ladies lavatory, and move swiftly from the enemy. In the high street the underground network are there to welcome me, not in words, or even glances, that would be giving the game away. It is our secret. Our mission. The Good must prevail for Him to enter the world again and redeem it. The old match seller outside the underground station smiles. He is truly blind. But he recognises the sound of my steps. I pause for breath, the traffic slows down. I am led into a shop. My hands reach for things quickly; food that will take care of us for a few days. I have never stolen before, but now it is my right, and I put the packages in my bag, not furtively, but quite openly, no one pays any attention. Even so I have to be careful for if the Manager sees the enemy watching then he has to say something. I pay for a few items only. The rest is piled high in my bag, but the weight is hardly anything, and my body feels warmer than it did in the coat.

I enter a Controlled Zone and slow down. A half demolished church. Dust and the musty smell of past incense and candle wax pervade the place. Small chipped statues of the stations of the cross line the crumbling walls. Wind howls through broken stained glass windows. Sound of pagan feet on the altar steps. Shadow of a leaning cross covers half of Satan's grinning face. Scuttle of those inhabiting the form of rats under slabs of grey stone. Merlin's magic staff beats the walls and commands me to go.

Walking back through a smaller park I climb through leaves. I feel as though I am scaling a waterfall. Those bloody Russian agents are everywhere, women pushing prams with monstrous dummy babies in them. Merlin in disguise waits near the fountain. He faces the sun; his shadow is a sun-dial thinness. Obviously I am not destined to go home yet, for I am led out of the park. It is to side-track the enemy, for I have lost them now.

I enter a museum; at last I can sit down, but no, a white-haired old man steps by and I have to follow him through winding corridors, in and out of rooms filled with tapestries. Finally into roped off areas depicting rooms of past centuries. Rooms I have known well, stuffy, hemmed in. Rooms where I half existed; rooms where I was betrayed; chairs I sat on and spun out dreams never to be realised; beds where generation after generation I was born, loved, gave birth, died in and born again. The old man pauses in front of each room, and he seems to chuckle.

'Stuffy in here isn't it?' He suddenly says, and turns round, then marches out. The first time any one of the underground movement has spoken to me. Not that I wish they spoke, but trying to mind-read the whole time gets exhausting. But I must get out of these ancient haunting times, the staleness is suffocating.

In the foyer a fat Russian woman agent pretends to look at the cards, and as I pass she pretends to accidentally bump into me. My God I must be careful, another incident like that could be the end; a small jab with a needle, and I would be in their hands. The woman follows me. I jump on to a bus, she sits next to me. The more I move away the closer she edges her monstrous body nearer. I quickly get off the bus and enter a huge department store. At least I have waylaid that one, but there are others in the store, pretending to look at things. I wish I could disguise myself, but I have tried that, wearing different clothes, sun glasses, a scarf, but it is hopeless; their mind reading computer is well programmed for any variation. I have to be careful too about where I might eat, drink and what I take. In fact it is such a risk eating out that I never do now. And then the cost of it; how I despise my previous way of life, allowing Clive to pay six or seven pounds for poisonous food. How on earth do I get out of this grotesque place, the way in was so easy? Escalators going up, but there seem to be none going down. They trap you in places like this, and the agents are everywhere, even the sales assistants have been warned.

If I get an entirely new outfit perhaps then I will not be detected? I have never before attempted stealing clothes, and my hands tremble as I put on a dress quickly, covered by my own clothes – isn't that how they do it? I'm done for if there are secret TV screening detectors. But I manage to get away with it, at least until I reach the pavement outside, where I am stopped by a uniformed attendant.

'Madam will you step inside please – we would like to see the receipts for what you have.' I manage to release his hand from my arm and run up the street into the cover of an underground station, where I go into the ladies, and later emerge in the new clothes, with the labels torn off, my old clothes left for some poor beggar no doubt. Ah well all for a good cause. And on with the journey; will I be recognised now? Possibly not at first, but it will not take long before they catch me out. It is beginning to rain as I enter the park once more. I hungrily drink the milk I pinched from a doorstep, and look round. The park is practically deserted, just a few park keepers brushing leaves, and soon the rain drives them away.

My new outfit is drenched through, and I am shivering, more through exhaustion than coldness. Can I get back now safely? The way through the park seems clear. But in the distance I hear the warning signal of an ambulance, and soon overhead an aeroplane flashes its red lights. Sure enough that woman agent awaits me on the path leading out of the park. There is nothing for it but to climb over the railings and take a devious route out. A peacock's cry signals that this is the right way, and other birds fly from branch to branch showing me the way through the undergrowth. The trees are so thick that they provide shelter from the rain, but the journey is difficult, over mounds of those buried, of those unable to find release, and I hear their cries with every step I take. At last I arrive at the edge of the park, and climb over the railings. No one about. All is quiet save for the dripping of rain on leaves and concrete, and the sound of city traffic beyond high walls.

Finally I reach the flat and lie down. My head spins. Automatically I look at the wall, but no face is there. I was granted just one vision of God, and that I must hold to. Nothing can be taken for granted any longer, even this flat, where I felt secure before. I must soon leave; the whole place is bugged. I must switch off the electricity, take the phone off the hook. But where shall I go? Do not question. And what of Clive? First you must go on with your journey, without him. Take all my savings out of the bank. Tomorrow I shall leave. No one must know. But first switch off the mains, then they will be less likely to detect my movements.

The rain has stopped, but they have not stopped searching for me. Two agents with an Alsatian dog walk by; ah how they pretend to be unassuming. A red car now parked outside the house, wired in to my radio – well I won't switch that on. I sit in the gathering darkness, hypnotised like a snake before the jets of flame and the sounds of the gas fire. Three candles are lit, two have steady fingers of light, one trembles. Clive is on his way back. How can I tell him – explain about switching off the mains? But of course, everything falls into place, he will not be coming back tonight, he stays in the country for an evening's teaching session. Look after him well spirits of the night. And yes they are here, three loud bangs from the gas fire prove that they have heard me.

My hands are directed to certain books, which I arrange in a circle as directed, opened not at random, but from their choice, or the way the wind blows through the half open window. It takes me a long time to read now, a paragraph holds so much significance, and everything links up. Soon I pick up the signal that it is Ireland I must go to, release the spirits of my ancestors in that country, and from there? But first things first, I must obviously not question further.

I move into my animal sleep, where my body sleeps, but my eyes remain open. Two hours suffice, and I am wide awake for the rest of the night. No time now spent in dreaming, for everything that happens and has happened is realised fully, no longer hidden in some strata of the unconscious.

A full moon cradled by the trees calls me out into the gardens. I hear the light of the stars, and feel the colour of the west wind forcing the shape of branches.

The spirits of the oak tree protect me from those struggling in their prisons from inferior trees.

My right side bids me leave and go into the street, but there are shadows lurking from doorways. Where can I hide? I dare not go back to the flat, they will only follow me. I try a car door, it opens. I climb in. It reeks of tobacco and beer. I have made a mistake, a murder has taken place in this car. They have trapped me. They will interrogate me, they will use me and then I will be executed. But I am saved, a police car appears on the corner, and blinks its lights. The shadows move back. It is safe to get out of this car. Return to the safety of the gardens. I have to be so careful, a little thing like that and I am lost, the world is lost.

I sink back against the oak tree and float up into the Milky Way. But the wind forces me out of the gardens once more, and into quiet back streets, where only cats are disturbed by my presence, and perhaps my steps echo in someone's dreams. I go towards the North Star. How quickly I can move at night, as though I am flying through the city. A city I am only now discovering. Territories that have been taken over by the enemy are in complete darkness; those of the underground movement always have a light showing, and these I keep close to, for I have found that it is painful moving in the enemy areas, their forces pull me back. At the end of the street a man waits in a car, moving slowly now towards me. I shuffle by in the disguise of an old tramp woman, but it does not fool him, he knows, and slowly pursues me.

The sound of wheels hissing on the asphalt, getting near and nearer. I hide in the hallway of a block of flats, until I hear the car move away.

I have no idea where I am, some unknown street, but the North Star is there. The engine throbbing warns me that the car is still waiting round the corner. The panic is so bad now that I even consider the idea of knocking up one of the underground movement people, but I cannot betray any one, and besides they would only pretend they didn't know, couldn't help, pretend I was some mad woman and call the police who in turn would carry out some pretence of officialdom. I must get back. But how? I do not even know where I am. Make a run for it that is the only way,

I stumble out and run down back streets, until I reach the main road, which I recognise. But the going is heavy, painful, I can hardly breathe, for I am in an area where the Zone ends. Now there are more cars hissing along, headlights blinding me from all directions. I want to get back to the flat – oh God please help me, let me go home. But you have no home, these commonplace little safety-valves must be liquidated, you are no longer a child, so stop behaving like one. And I am behaving like a child, stranded, no one to turn to.

On an island where either side of me evil forces are speeding by in their monstrous machines. I am not breathing properly, damn it my lungs are in poor shape, all those years of nicotine and tar; if I hold my breath then the cars will slow down and I can get across to the other side. Like underwater I manage it, and gasping for air I turn into some more back streets. Obviously it is too dangerous for me to return to the flat, will I have to put up at a hotel? Wait a minute there are some friends nearby, though they are more Clive's friends than mine, but still…

'Sandra what on earth's the matter – are you all right?'

'I'm being followed quick let me in.'

'Followed by whom?'

'Don't laugh but I'm being followed by Russian spies.'

'You better come in and tell us all about it – want to stay the night here?'

ONE DAY IN THE LIFE OF A WRITER

Woke up from dream of my publisher handing me a cheque, to the post – letter from my publisher regret Arts Council have refused a grant, no reason given... That's 'cos they read what I did with the last one. Ah well on to a passable crap. Retreat into ex-tenant's room to write, confronted by a little heap of dust, bugs, etc., landlady has brushed up, cursing I put into dustpan to the sound of 'do you want some coffee now or later are you warm enough in there what do you want for lunch there's kippers, lamb stew, eggs or bacon or...?'. Close door and confront blank paper in typewriter. Look at some notes made from Harry Guntrip's book on Schizoid Phenomena, Object Relations and the Self. 'Patients become inaccessible emotionally, when the patient seems to be bodily present but mentally absent.' 'I went down into a tower and then had to go through a tunnel to get out. Though I had come in that way I was horrified.' 'The symptoms were a defence against guilt and depression about his hostility to his mother. He was orally dependent on her. In this connexion it is significant that he sucked his thumb all his life.' I start my round of oral masturbation with a cigarette. Window cleaner props ladder outside and stares in. Re-start novel; finally get the tone right, decide that's the most important part of it all: the tone.

Lunch. Walkies along the Front with Mother. We sit down. 'Look at that it looks like a Martian look he's coming to get you – ' Umhhhh? A large piece of shitty paper bounces along. 'Oh God he's coming to sit next to us come on dear let's move.' Ummhhh? 'No thank God he's decided to sit next to them.'

Library – practically empty except for the section I want. The usual eccentric-looking fraternity gathered around the Psychology section.

Open a book on Hostility and read 'You can guess what happened, if you do not already know. In the wee hours of the morning Stretch would tiptoe to the door of the guest room, open it ever so softly, and peek in, just to make sure. You can also guess what he saw and what utter consternation seized him at finding his guest either too short or too long – never a perfect fit. And now, knowing how it was that Stretch was trying so hard to be a perfect host, it is quite easy to see that next he simply had to do what he did.' Back along the Front where Bergy men furtively walk, sit, spit and mutter.

Back home and nice tea dear. Start decorating and spend most of the time wiping off emulsion drops from parquet flooring, burn hole in carpet from cigarette, burn hole in table lampshade. Give up in despair and foul temper. Back to writing the tone is all wrong. I'm no

longer capable of writing that's why the Arts Council —
they know you know. Watch tele. Watch myself watching and being watched by Mother in between her sleep,
and hear her shudder as an old woman comes on. And
so to bed.

A NOTE ON SOURCES

Since Ann Quin's death in 1973, her papers have remained scattered across archives and private collections. The stories and fragments collected in this volume were gathered from the Calder and Boyars Manuscript Collection at the Lilly Library, Indiana University and from the private collections of her friends, the writer Carol Burns and Fr. Brocard Sewell in London, the poet Larry Goodell from New Mexico, the New Zealand Pop artist, Billy Apple. I would like to extend my thanks to all the above, as well as Meg Randall of *El Corno Emplumado*, the staff of the Washington State University Archives, Jane Percival, Robert Sward, Richard Copsey and Tina Barton for their help in locating and collecting these stories.

Throughout this collection, I've tried to retain the integrity of Quin's original text. I've corrected spelling, grammatical and typographical errors where they weren't intended stylistically. The stories are presented more or less in chronological order, except where shared thematic concerns seemed to call for them to be grouped together.

'Leaving School – XI' was first published in the *London Magazine* 4 (July 1966).

'Nude and Seascape' is previously unpublished, undated, and from the Fr. Brocard Sewell archive at the Carmelite Friary in East Finchley, London.

'A Double Room' is previously unpublished, was written ca. 1966 (as mentioned in the author's correspondence with Marion Boyars), and is from the private collection of Larry Goodell.

'Every Cripple Has His Own Way of Walking' was first published in *Nova* (December 1966).

'B.B.'s Second Manifesto' is from the private collection of Billy Apple and was ghostwritten for Billy Apple, ca. 1962.

'Untitled (Neh Man It's Like This)' is from the private collection of Billy Apple and was also ghostwritten for Billy Apple, ca. 1962.

'Living in the Present' (co-written with Robert Sward) was first published in *Ambit* 34 (1968) and is published here with permission of Robert Sward.

'Tripticks' was first published in *Ambit* 35 (1968).

'Never Trust a Man Who Bathes With His Fingernails' was first published in *El Corno Emplumado* 27 (July 1968).

'Eyes That Watch Behind the Wind' was first published in *A Signature Anthology* (Calder and Boyars, 1975), and was written in 1968.

'Ghostworm' was first published in *Tak Tak Tak* 6 (1993), and was written in 1969.

'Motherlogue' was first published in *Transatlantic Review* 32 (1969), and was written ca. 1969.

'The Unmapped Country' is previously unpublished and from the Lilly Library Calder and Boyars Manuscript Collection and the Fr. Brocard Sewell archive. It is unfinished and was written in 1973.

'One Day in the Life of a Writer' is previously unpublished, from the private collection of Carol Burns, and has not been dated.

Dear readers,

As well as relying on bookshop sales, And Other Stories relies on subscriptions from people like you for many of our books, whose stories other publishers often consider too risky to take on.

Our subscribers don't just make the books physically happen. They also help us approach booksellers, because we can demonstrate that our books already have readers and fans. And they give us the security to publish in line with our values, which are collaborative, imaginative and 'shamelessly literary'.

All of our subscribers:

- receive a first-edition copy of each of the books they subscribe to
- are thanked by name at the end of our subscriber-supported books
- receive little extras from us by way of thank you, for example: postcards created by our authors

BECOME A SUBSCRIBER, OR GIVE A SUBSCRIPTION TO A FRIEND

Visit andotherstories.org/subscribe to help make our books happen. You can subscribe to books we're in the process of making. To purchase books we have already published, we urge you to support your local or favourite bookshop and order directly from them – the often unsung heroes of publishing.

OTHER WAYS TO GET INVOLVED

If you'd like to know about upcoming events and reading groups (our foreign-language reading groups help us choose books to publish, for example) you can:

- join the mailing list at: andotherstories.org/join-us
- follow us on Twitter: @andothertweets
- join us on Facebook: facebook.com/AndOtherStoriesBooks
- follow our blog: andotherstoriespublishing.tumblr.com

This book was made possible thanks to the support of:

Aaron McEnery · Aaron Schneider · Ada Gokay · Adam Barnard · Adam Bowman · Adam Guy · Adam Lenson · Adriana Diaz Enciso · Agata Rucinska · Aifric Ni Chathmhaoil · Aileen-Elizabeth Taylor · Ailsa Peate · Aisling Reina · Ajay Sharma · Alan Donnelly · Alan McMonagle · Alasdair Hutchison · Alastair Gillespie · Alex Hancock · Alex Ramsey · Alex Robertson · Alexandra Citron · Alexia Richardson · Alfred Birnbaum · Ali Conway · Ali MacKenzie · Ali Smith · Alice Ramsey · Alison Layland · Alison MacConnell · Alison Winston · Alyse Ceirante · AM Stripe · Amanda · Amanda Astley · Amanda Harvey · Amber Da · Amelia Ashton · Amelia Dowe · Amine Hamadache · Amitav Hajra · Amy Rushton · Ana Hincapie · Andrea Reece · Andrew Gummerson · Andrew Marston · Andrew McCallum · Andrew Rego · Angela Everitt · Angharad Jones · Anna-Maria Aurich · Anna Dowrick · Anna Glendenning · Anna Johnson · Anna McKee-Poore · Anna Milsom · Anne Carus · Anne Frost · Anne Guest · Anne Stokes · Anneliese O'Malley · Anonymous · Anonymous · Anonymous · Anthony Brown · Anthony McGuinness · Anthony Quinn · Anton Muscatelli · Antonia Lloyd-Jones · Antonia Saske · Antonio de Swift · Antony Pearce · Aoife Boyd · Archie Davies · Arwen Smith · Asako Serizawa · Asher Norris · Ashley Hamilton · Audrey Mash · Avril Marren · Barbara Mellor · Barbara & Terry Feller · Barry John Fletcher · Bella Besong · Ben Schofield · Ben Thornton · Benjamin Judge · Beth Hancock · Beth O'Neill · Bettina Rogerson · Beverly Jackson · Bianca Duec · Bianca Jackson · Bianca Winter · Bill Fletcher · Blythe Ridge Sloan · Branka Maricic · Brenda Sully · Briallen Hopper · Brigid O'Connor · Brigita Ptackova · Caitlin Halpern · Caitlin Liebenberg · Caitlyn Chappell · Caitriona Lally · Callie Steven · Cam Scott · Candida Lacey · Carl Emery · Carol Laurent · Carol Mavor · Carol McKay · Carolina Pineiro · Caroline Maldonado · Caroline Picard · Caroline Smith · Caroline Waight · Caroline West · Cassidy Hughes · Catharine Mee · Catherine Lambert · Catherine Taylor · Catriona Gibbs · Cecilia Rossi · Cecilia Uribe · Cecily Maude · Ceri Webb · Charles Raby · Charlotte Holtam · Charlotte Middleton · Charlotte Murrie & Stephen Charles · Charlotte Ryland · Charlotte Whittle · Chenxin Jiang · Chia Foon Yeow · China Miéville · Chris Ames · Chris Gribble · Chris Hughes · Chris Lintott · Chris McCann · Chris & Kathleen Repper-Day · Chris Stevenson · Christina Moutsou · Christine Brantingham · Christine Luker · Christopher Allen · Christopher Terry · Ciara Ní Riain · Claire Allison · Claire Brooksby · Claire Malcolm · Claire Riley · Claire Tristram · Claire Williams · Clare Archibald · Clarice Borges · Clarice Borges · Clarissa Botsford · Claudia Hoare · Claudia Nannini · Clifford Posner · Clive Bellingham · Clive Hewat · Colin Burrow · Colin Matthews · Corey Nelson · Courtney Lilly · Csilla Toldy · Dan Walpole · Daniel Arnold · Daniel Coxon · Daniel Douglas · Daniel Gallimore · Daniel Gillespie · Daniel Hahn · Daniel Rice · Daniel Stewart · Daniel Sweeney · Daniela Steierberg · Dave Lander · Davi Rocha · David Anderson · David Finlay · David Gavin · David Hebblethwaite · David Higgins · David Johnson-Davies · David Jones · David F Long · David Mantero · David Miller · David Shriver · David Smith · David Steege · David Travis · Debbie Pinfold · Declan O'Driscoll · Deirdre Nic Mhathuna · Denis

Larose · Denis Stillewagt & Anca Fronescu · Diana Fox Carney · Dinah Bourne · Dominick Santa Cattarina · Dominique Brocard · Duncan Clubb · Duncan Marks · E Rodgers · Edward Haxton · Elaine Rassaby · Eleanor Dawson · Eleanor Maier · Elie Howe · Elina Zicmane · Elisabeth Cook · Eliza O'Toole · Elizabeth Cochrane · Ellen Coopersmith · Ellen Jones · Ellen Kennedy · Ellen Wilkinson · Elly Zelda Goldsmith · Emily Chia & Marc Ronnie · Emily Taylor · Emily Yaewon Lee & Gregory Limpens · Emma Barraclough · Emma Bielecki · Emma Louise Grove · Emma Perry · Emma Teale · Emma Yearwood · Erin Braybrook · Eva Kostyu · Ewan Tant · Filiz Emre-Cooke · Finbarr Farragher · Finlay McEwan · Fiona Quinn · Florian Duijsens · Fran Sanderson · Francesca Brooks · Francesca Fanucci · Francis Taylor · Friederike Knabe · Gabriela Lucia Garza de Linde · Gabrielle Crockatt · Gary Gorton · Gavin Smith · Gawain Espley · Gemma Tipton · Geoff Copps · Geoff Thrower · Geoffrey Cohen · Geoffrey Urland · George Christie · George Hawthorne · George McCaig · George Wilkinson · Georgia Panteli · Gill Boag-Munroe · Gillian Bohnet · Gillian Grant · Gillian Spencer · Gordon Cameron · Graham R

Foster · Guy Haslam · Hadil Balzan · Hank Pryor · Hannah Mayblin · Hannah Richter · Hannah Stevens · Hans Lazda · Harriet Mossop · Helen Barker · Helen Brady · Helen Collins · Helen Gough · Helen Snow · Helen Swain · Helen White · Henrike Laehnemann · Henry Asson · Henry Patino · Hilary McGrath · Howard Robinson · Hugh Gilmore · Iain Munro · Ian Barnett · Ian McMillan · Ian Smith · Íde Corley · Ingrid Olsen · Irene Mansfield · Irina Tzanova · Isabel Adey · Isabella Livorni · Isabella Weibrecht · J Collins · Jacinta Perez Gavilan Torres · Jack Brown · Jacqueline Lademann · Jacqueline Ting Lin · Jacqueline Vint · James Beck · James Couling · James Crossley · James Cubbon · James Lesniak · James Mewis · James Portlock · James Scudamore · James Tierney · James Ward · Jamie Mollart · Jamie Osborn · Jamie Walsh · Jane Leuchter · Jane Mark-Lawson · Jane Woollard · Janette Ryan · Janne Støen · Jasmine Gideon · JC Sutcliffe · Jean-Jacques Regouffre · Jeff Collins · Jeffrey Davies · Jennifer Bernstein · Jennifer Harvey · Jennifer Higgins · Jennifer O'Brien · Jenny Booth · Jenny Huth · Jenny Newton · Jenny Nicholls · Jeremy Faulk · Jeremy Koenig · Jeremy Morton · Jeremy Weinstock ·

Jerry Simcock · Jess Howard-Armitage · Jessica Billington · Jessica Kibler · Jethro Soutar · Jim Boucherat · Jo Bell · Jo Harding · Jo Lateu · Joan O'Malley · Joanna Flower · Joanna Luloff · Joao Pedro Bragatti Winckler · Jodie Adams · Joel Love · Joelle Skilbeck · Johan Forsell · Johan Trouw · Johanna Eliasson · Johannes Menzel · John Berube · John Conway · John Coyne · John Down · John Gent · John Hodgson · John Kelly · John McGill · John McKee · John Royley · John Shaw · John Steigerwald · John Winkelman · Jon Riches · Jon Talbot · Jonathan Blaney · Jonathan Jackson · Jonathan Kiehlmann · Jonathan Ruppin · Jonathan Watkiss · Joseph Cooney · Joseph Huennekens · Joseph Schreiber · Joshua Davis · Joshua McNamara · Judith Martens · Julia Hays · Julia Hobsbawm · Julian Duplain · Julian Lomas · Juliana Giraldo · Julie Gibson · Julie Gibson · Julie-Ann Griffiths · Juliet Swann · JW Mersky · Kaarina Hollo · Karen Faarbaek de Andrade Lima · Karen Waloschek · Kasim Husain · Kasper Haakansson · Kasper Hartmann · Kate Attwooll · Kate Gardner · Kate Griffin · Katharina Becker · Katharina Liehr · Katharine Freeman · Katharine Robbins · Katherine El-Salahi · Katherine Mackinnon ·

Katherine Skala · Kathleen Magone · Kathryn Edwards · Kathryn Lewis · Katie Brown · Katrina Thomas · Katya Zotova · Kay Warbrick · Kent McKernan · Kevin Porter · Khairunnisa Ibrahim · Kirsten Major · KL Ee · Klara Rešetič · Kristin Djuve · Krystine Phelps · Lana Selby · Lander Hawes · Laura Batatota · Laura Clarke · Laura Lea · Lauren Ellemore · Laurence Laluyaux · Laurie Sheck & Jim Peck · Leeanne O'Neill · Leon Frey · Leonie Schwab · Leonie Smith · Lesley Lawn · Lesley Watters · Leslie Wines · Liam Fleming · Liliana Lobato · Lily Levinson · Lindsay Brammer · Lindsey Ford · Lisa Edelbacher · Liz Ketch · Lizzie Broadbent · Lizzie Coulter · Lochlan Bloom · Loretta Platts · Lorna Bleach · Lorraine Bramwell · Lottie Smith · Louise Curtin · Louise Musson · Louise Piper · Luc Verstraete · Lucia Rotheray · Lucy Moffatt · Lucy Phillips · Lucy Summers · Luke Williamson · Lynda Graham · Lynn Martin · M Manfre · Madeline Teevan · Maeve Lambe · Maggie Humm · Maggie Redway · Mahan L Ellison & K Ashley Dickson · Manja Pflanz · Marcella Morgan · Margaret Briggs · Margaret Jull Costa · Marie Bagley · Marie Cloutier · Marie Donnelly · Marina Castledine · Marina Galanti · Marina Jones · Mark Dawson · Mark Lumley · Mark Sargent · Mark & Sarah Sheets · Mark Sztyber · Mark Waters · Marlene Adkins · Martha Gifford · Martha Nicholson · Martha Stevns · Martin Boddy · Martin Nathan · Martin Vosyka · Martin Whelton · Mary Carozza · Mary Wang · Marzieh Youssefi · Matt & Owen Davies · Matt Klein · Matthew Armstrong · Matthew Black · Matthew Francis · Matthew Geden · Matthew Smith · Matthew Thomas · Matthew Warshauer · Matthew Woodman · Matty Ross · Maureen Pritchard · Max Cairnduff · Max Longman · Maxim Grigoriev · Meaghan Delahunt · Megan Wittling · Meike Schwamborn · Melissa Beck · Melissa Quignon-Finch · Meredith Jones · Meredith Martin · Merima Jahic · Meryl Wingfield · Michael Andal · Michael James Eastwood · Michael Gavin · Michael Johnston · Michael Moran · Michele Keyaert · Michelle Lotherington · Michelle Roberts · Mike Bittner · Mike Timms · Milo Waterfield · Miranda Gold · Miranda Persaud · Molly Foster · Monica Anderson · Monika Olsen · Morag Campbell · Morgan Lyons · Myles Nolan · N Tsolak · Namita Chakrabarty · Nancy Oakes · Natalie Smith · Natalie Steer · Nathalie Atkinson · Nathan Dorr · Navi Sahota · Ned Vaught · Neil Pretty · Nicholas Brown · Nick Chapman · Nick Flegel · Nick James · Nick Nelson & Rachel Eley · Nick Sidwell · Nicola Hart · Nicola Mira · Nicola Sandiford · Nicole Matteini · Nigel Palmer · Nikki Brice · Nikki Sinclair · Nikolaj Ramsdal Nielsen · Nina Alexandersen · Nina Moore · Nina Power · Noah Levin · Noelle Harrison · Octavia Kingsley · Olga Alexandru · Olga Zilberbourg · Olivia Payne · Pam Madigan · Pamela Ritchie · Pashmina Murthy · Patricia Appleyard · Patricia Hughes · Patrick McGuinness · Paul Bailey · Paul Cray · Paul Daw · Paul Griffiths · Paul Howe & Ally Hewitt · Paul Jones · Paul Munday · Paul Myatt · Paul Segal · Paula Edwards · Penelope Hewett Brown · Perlita Payne · Pete Stephens · Peter McCambridge · Peter Rowland · Peter Vilbig · Peter Vos · Philip Carter · Philip Warren · Philippa Wentzel · Piet Van Bockstal · PRAH Foundation · Rachael Williams · Rachel Barnes · Rachel Carter · Rachel Hinkel · Rachel Lasserson · Rachel Van Riel · Rachel Watkins · Rachele Huennekens · Rea Cris · Rebecca Braun · Rebecca Carter · Rebecca Moss · Rebecca Rosenthal · Rebekah

Hughes · Réjane Collard-Walker · Rhiannon Armstrong · Rhodri Jones · Richard Ashcroft · Richard Bauer · Richard John Davis · Richard Dew · Richard Gwyn · Richard Harrison · Richard Mansell · Richard Priest · Richard Shea · Richard Shore · Richard Soundy · Rita Hynes · Robert Downing · Robert Gillett · Robert Norman · Roberta Allport · Robin Patterson · Robin Taylor · Roger Salloch · Ronan Cormacain · Rory Williamson · Rosanna Foster · Rose Arnold · Rowena McWilliams · Roxanne O'Del Ablett · Royston Tester · Roz Simpson · Rune Salvesen · Rupert Ziziros · S Wight · Sabrina Uswak · Sally Baker · Sally Dowell · Sam Gordon · Sam Norman · Sam Reese · Sam Ruddock · Sam Stern · Samantha Smith · Sandra Mayer · Sarah Arboleda · Sarah Benson · Sarah Butler · Sarah Jacobs · Sarah Lucas · Sarah Pybus · Sarah Wollner · Scott Thorough · Sean Kelly · Sean Malone · Sean McGivern · Sean Stewart · Sez Kiss · Shannon Beckner · Shannon Knapp · Shaun Whiteside · Shauna Gilligan · Shawn Moedl · Sheridan Marshall · Shira Lob · Shirley Harwood · Sian O'Neill · Sian Rowe · Silvia Kwon · Simon Armstrong · Simon Clark · Simon Robertson · Simone O'Donovan · SK Grout · Sofia Mostaghimi · Sonia Crites · Sonia McLintock · Sophia Wickham · Soren Murhart · ST Dabbagh · Stacy Rodgers · Stefanie May IV · Stefano Mula · Steph Morris · Stephan Eggum · Stephanie Lacava · Stephen Coade · Stephen Eisenhammer · Stephen Pearsall · Steve Ford · Steven & Gitte Evans · Stu Sherman · Stuart Wilkinson · Sue Little · Susan Higson · Susan Manser · Susie Roberson · Suzanne Fortey · Suzanne Lee · Swannee Welsh · Sylvie Zannier-Betts · Tamara Larsen · Tammi Owens · Tammy Watchorn · Tania Hershman · Ted Burness · Teresa Griffiths · Terry Kurgan · Terry Woodward · The Mighty Douche Softball Team · The Rookery In the Bookery · Thees Spreckelsen · Therese Oulton · Thomas Bell · Thomas Chadwick · Thomas Fritz · Thomas Mitchell · Thomas van den Bout · Tiffany Lehr · Tim Theroux · Timothy Harris · Tina Rotherham-Winqvist · TJ Clark · Toby Ryan · Tom Darby · Tom Franklin · Tom Gray · Tom Whatmore · Tom Wilbey · Tony Bastow · Tony Messenger · Torna Russell-Hills · Tory Jeffay · Tracy Bauld · Tracy Heuring · Tracy Lee-Newman · Tracy Northup · Tracy Shapley · Trevor Lewis · Trevor Wald · Val Challen · Valerie Hamra · Vanessa Dodd · Vanessa Nolan · Veronica Cockburn · Victor Meadowcroft · Victoria Adams · Victoria Maitland · Victoria Seaman · Victoria Smith · Vijay Pattisapu · Vikki O'Neill · Virginia Weir · Visaly Muthusamy · Wendy Langridge · Wendy Olson · Wendy Peate · Wenna Price · Will Huxter · William Dennehy · William Schwaber · William Schwartz · Zoe Stephenson · Zoe Thomas · Zoë Brasier ·

Current & Upcoming Books

ANN QUIN was a British writer, born in Brighton in 1936. Prior to her death in 1973, she published four novels: *Berg* (1964), *Three* (1966), *Passages* (1969) and *Tripticks* (1972). During her writing career, she lived between Brighton, London and the United States. She was prominent amongst a group of British experimental writers of the 1960s, which also included BS Johnson and Christine Brooke-Rose.

JENNIFER HODGSON is a writer and critic from Hull. She writes about literature and culture for a variety of publications, including *The Guardian* and *The White Review*, and is currently writing the first critical study of Ann Quin's work. She was previously UK Editor at Dalkey Archive Press.